LOST & FOUND

AN IRISH MYSTICAL ROMANCE

PENELOPE JEAN BLISS

Published in the United States by Bend in the Road Press, Brownsville, VT.

Trade paperback ISBN: 9781736455111

This is a work of fiction. All characters, names, places and events (past and present) are products of my imagination. Any resemblance to actual people, places or events is coincidental.

Cover illustration by Miblart.

"The world is full of magic things patiently waiting
for our senses to grow sharper."
W B Yeats

NOW

Usually, it was tea for just two. Today it could be tea for three, or perhaps four. Maddy closed her eyes and concentrated, centering herself to see what might come. Sometimes she could sense these things, but she felt nothing, no sign to let her know how many guests to expect. Best to get out four cups just in case. There was comfort in the routine, the structure and normalcy of serving tea.

The hot water was poured into the pot to warm it up with a tea cozy neatly tucked over it to keep it at the perfect temperature until it was time. The pot would be emptied, and fresh boiling water and tea leaves would be added after their guests arrived. The pre-warmed pot would keep it all at just the right temperature for a wee bit longer, getting the most flavor out of the delicate tea leaves. Ginger scones would be coming out of the oven soon and would be tucked in a linen cloth in the seagrass basket her friend Nora had made. Fresh butter was already in the dish, and pots of homemade lavender jelly and honey were on the table.

Madeline Murphy was born with the sight. Not an easy thing growing up, as the adults in her early life didn't understand that sometimes she just knew things that were going to happen. Some laughed it off, some were angry, and some afraid. She never knew her da. When asked, her mum would say he was a bum, a right royal shit, a bastard, a coward or worse, but never who he actually was. Sometimes she'd look Maddy in the eye and say, not kindly, that she was spawn of the devil himself, had his look about her, and wasn't that a shame. Her mum might truly not have known who fathered her, as she could barely see past her own needs day to day, let alone understand how it was that Maddy could 'see' things that weren't there, that hadn't happened yet.

At the age of four, she mentioned to her mum that they should leave before the Garda arrived to arrest the man living with them. The man fled, but not before Maddy was punished for not keeping her mouth shut. Then, with the earnestness and innocence of childhood, she'd asked who the other woman was who was sleeping in her mum's bed. That had caused a major fall out, and there was hell to pay for months. Maddy soon learned to keep her visions and dreams to herself, but even in transient urban slums, gossip got around. Word of Maddy's peculiar talents piqued the notice of a few men with peculiar interests. They wanted to control and exploit. Her mum, Frannie, didn't take this well. It wasn't so much concern about her daughter's welfare, but rather the male attention she was receiving.

There was unwanted attention on all sides, as representatives of child services were also watching. Frannie's boyfriends were paying more attention to the daughter rather than her mum. These men often showed more interest in what Maddy might do for them, might *see* for them. They took the young girl to horse races and to the pub to lay odds on sports games, with Frannie tagging along as an afterthought.

Finally, Frannie had had enough. When Maddy was eight, a few of her things were hastily tossed in a battered duffle, then she bundled the girl into the back seat of a boyfriend's car, drove to the West Coast and abruptly, unceremoniously, dumped her at her Gran's door. Maddy remembered Gran coming out, wiping her hands on a faded pink apron. Frannie hadn't been back home to the West Coast in years. They hadn't said but a handful of words to each other in all those years. Suddenly appearing on the doorstep, with nary a warning nor a greeting, she simply got out of the car, gestured and yelled. "Here, take her. Her name's Madeline. She's a bother and a pest. Saints know I've done my best, but she's hopeless."

With that, Frannie tossed the battered duffle and a bulging pillowcase at Maddy's feet, climbed back in the car, turned and sped down the lane back to Dublin. Gran hadn't said a word, but came down the steps and opened her arms wide, enveloping Maddy in a welcoming hug. The girl was thin, scared and silent. Annie Donahue had never been able to understand nor reach her own daughter, mend what ailed her, but she would see to the tending and mending of her granddaughter.

"Welcome Madeline," Gran had said, softly.

"Maddy," she corrected. "Sometimes she calls me Baddy Maddy," came a whispered confession.

"Well, Maddy 'tis then. But nothing bad about you, now is there? Let's go in and see about some tea, shall we?"

Maddy liked the way this woman smelled. She liked her soft hands and gentle voice. All foreign to her, but intriguing nonetheless. She vowed silently to be on her best behavior and not mention any visions or dreams. Then maybe she could stay.

The Irish western coast suited the young girl just fine. It had taken time, a gentle hand and patience, but Maddy gradually settled into routine, and with it came trust. Frannie and the constant uncertainties of her old life faded as the days went along. There was no word from Frannie, nor anyone from her previous existence. "No word, no worry," her Gran would say. Gran said that as she needed the help, clearly the good Lord had most likely sent her to help and so she did. Maddy loved learning how to tend the garden, do small errands when she could, and when old enough, baked sweets and breads for the local pub. She also bottled the honey from Gran's hives as her grandmother showed her, and eventually started her own cottage industry, with honey, jams, baked goods, seaweed soap and dried herbs to sell locally. The tourists had come now to look for 'Madeline's Magic' specialty items. They were so popular that some were even shipped to stores in Dublin.

Bit by bit Maddy came out of her shell, grew and blossomed. Slowly, carefully, like testing scalded milk with a finger, she shared her visions with the older woman. Small things at first, like a suggestion they take another route to the village for a change. It turned out Amos Bugsby's sheep had gotten out and had been blocking the road Gran usually took. Then she mentioned seeing newlywed parishoners with their baby boy. Six months later the couple welcomed young Seamus into the world. Her gift, as her Gran had taught her to think of her visions, were accepted as a valuable part of who she was. She'd done well in school, was an avid reader, and even made a few friends, but Maddy remained cautious about sharing her visions. Mostly she kept them to herself or on rare occasion shared them with her Gran.

She'd also learned the art of subtle hints, suggestions as it were, to friends or even strangers. Visitors to her friend Nora's shop had mentioned taking a particular road to historic ruins. Maddy overheard and suggested an alternate route, a scenic one that went past an old castle ruin not on the usual tourist maps. She'd heard later that they were thankful they didn't follow their original plans as there was an overturned lorry that had blocked the road for hours. Weren't they lucky Maddy had mentioned another route. Lucky? Yes. Maddy smiled.

Now she surveyed the parlor table, and nodded. Her nerves skittered a bit under her skin. The table was nearly ready, but was she? She took a deep breath. If asked, as she felt she would be, to open to her gift for her Gran's friend in need, well, she would do this, could do this, for her Gran. She would do almost anything for her Gran. It wasn't just gratitude, but a deep love for a woman who was more a mother to her than the woman who had given birth. Her Grandmother spoke little of Frannie, and when she did there was sorrow for a lost soul. Then, inevitably, she'd lay a soft hand on Maddy's cheek and say Maddy was the best thing Frannie left behind.

The woman coming today, perhaps with her companion, was an old school chum of her Gran's. They had exchanged Christmas and birthday cards since childhood, and there was the occasional short phone call. Still, when Mrs. Belinda O'Neill, nee O'Shea, called to say she needed help, Gran told her to come and talk to her granddaughter, Madeline. Maddy might be able to see what the problem was.

As she set out the fine china teacups and laid the sugar tongs on the small cut glass bowl of sugar cubes, Maddy sighed. Gran had assured her t'would be fine—Belinda had a good soul and an old one—she'd understand. Nerves still had her on edge. Oh dear, she thought, what had her Gran gotten her into?

It wasn't long before an ancient Mini Cooper pulled in. It came to a jolting halt, shuddered and settled. Two equally ancient ladies clambered out. Tweed hats perched just so, tweed suits buttoned neatly, substantial pocketbooks clutched under their arms. One reminded Madeline of the Queen, the other one of her corgis, short, stocky, with reddish hair, turning gray, following directly and obediently behind.

Opening the door just as they came slowly up the steps, Maddy greeted them with a warm welcome. "Good Morning ladies," she said brightly, ushering them in. "Please make yourselves at home. I've tea and scones in the parlor."

Madeline's Gran came in from the back garden, took off her gardening gloves and came over to give her long-time friend a hug. "Ah, 'tis good to see you my dear! You're looking very smart in that suit, all fancy and citified."

"Be gone with ya, Annie, I've had this suit for a dog's age and then some. You are just as full of the blarney as ever." This was said with a twinkle and a grin.

Belinda O'Neill then made introductions. "Annie, this is my friend, Clara O'Malley. Clara, this is Annie Donahue, my oldest school chum and keeper of all my secrets."

"Oh, tosh now my dear, I am sure you have plenty of secrets yet to share. Pleased to meet you, Clara. And, this is my granddaughter, Madeline. Come and sit, we'll have some tea and catch up a bit."

"I'm so glad you could join us." Maddy addressed both of the women in the entry hall. "Please call me Maddy. You can leave your things right here on the bench."

The four sat down to a lovely tea, exclaiming over the homemade scones, honey, lavender jelly, and fresh berries. The conversation bounced around from past memories to new gossip about distant friends and relations. Both Belinda and Clara lived in the same council housing for seniors in the small town of Ballrowan. It seems that life there was fraught with drama, soap operas and intrigue. Who was chatting up who, who had a knee replaced, whose sciatica had flared up, whose children were fighting in the parking lot, and on and on.

It finally came time for the business of their trip. Gran invited Clara to join her for a look at the garden to give her granddaughter and her friend a chance to chat alone.

Belinda and Maddy were left in the sunny parlor, the dishes set away in the kitchen.

"Well, my dear, Annie said I should bring something that has a connection to my troubles." With that, she dug into her cavernous pocketbook and pulled out an old marmalade jar of dirt.

"I think my neighbor, Mrs. Sullivan, soon to be Mrs. Dougherty, I'll have you know, is trying to kill my prize-winning roses so she will win the garden club award next year. My best in show, Moonlight pink rose, is being dug up and pulled almost out of the ground. The first time I simply re-planted it and added some more of my secret ingredient." She leaned in to whisper, although it was just the two of them in the parlor. "I get peat from a bog near Cloonmolly. Good for the soil, don't ya know... makes the blooms bigger, brighter and more fragrant." She sniffed loudly and beamed. "Ahh, the smell alone would win me the prize."

Then she frowned as she lifted the jar off the table, shaking it towards Maddy as she spoke. "But it has happened two more times! Torn up and tossed aside. I confronted her about it, but she denies it. Says I am making it up because I am jealous of her green thumb. As if I would ever! I suggested she needed to go confess her sins to Father Donovan, because lying is most certainly a sin. She had the nerve to say I was the one who should be sitting in the confessional, because false accusations were an even greater sin. Furthermore, I know she is sneaky..." Leaning in once again, voice hardened, she continued, "because Mr. Dougherty was setting his cap for sweet Clara, and the next thing you know," a finger jabbed the air, "Mrs. Sullivan lured him away with her bread pudding and flirty ways. You would think a man of eighty-eight would know better than to be taken in by a seventy-eight-year-old floozie, but he popped the question and she accepted. Rumor has it he wanted to move in with her, but she wouldn't 'live in sin,' and insisted they be married. Sneaky as the day is long, that one."

The jar of dirt was once again set on the table with a definitive *thunk*.

Maddy opened the lid carefully and tipped a bit of soil in her hand. "Well, let's see if it has anything to tell us." She closed her eyes, took a deep breath. There was the distinctive earthy, acrid smell of peat mixed in with the more subtle odor of the soil. She put her other hand over the cupped one and concentrated on the feel and essence. Like an image coming out of the fog, she started to make out a young dog, maybe a small dog rather than a young one. Maybe a terrier.

"Mrs. O'Neill, does someone in your neighborhood have a small terrier, or a puppy?"

"Oh yes, the young couple who manage the council houses now just got a pet for their little lad. When they are not to home, they keep it in the garden behind their flat."

Madeline tipped her handful back into the jar and dusted her hands off. "Well, I think you will find he is a very clever little fellow, and has probably dug himself a back door to the garden. He is getting out unattended and has found an interest in something under your roses. I would try spreading some small rocks around the base or try some orange peels—some dogs dislike the smell. The wee fella may be left alone too long and then he gets bored. You may want to let the owners know about the hole in their fence, and perhaps, if you are so inclined, bring a few dog toys or a nice bone to keep him busy. Better a new toy or bone than your rose bush."

Mrs. O'Neill looked a bit put out and disappointed for a minute. This was not the answer she had been thinking to hear. Ah well.

"Mrs. Sullivan is still not to be trusted." She winced and then said firmly, "but I will apologize to her for mistaking her for a dog."

Maddy held back a laugh at that. Clearly her Gran's friend had had the wind plucked out of her indignant sails. As they stood up to meet the other two in the garden, Maddy realized that the hand that had held the dirt was still tingling, and there was another image just on the fringes of her mind. It was much, much older and darker, and not quite discernible.

On impulse she picked up the jar. "Here, let me take care of this for you. I think you will find the mystery is solved, and if not, I'll hang on to the evidence and try again. Just let Gran know." She set the jar carefully on the mantel over the small coal fireplace, next to the vase of lavender and the cheeky wooden leprechaun with a faded label stating it was a souvenir from Tipperary.

There the jar sat, quietly, patiently. Madeline would catch it out of the corner of her eye as she passed the fireplace. Whatever mystery was in there had waited a long time already. It would need to wait a bit longer. She sensed it waiting, wanting, calling out to her. *Soon*, she'd answer, *soon*.

NOW

Vivid dreams often came with the territory, she supposed. Often they'd be sharper, more emotion-laden, more absorbing than the usual flotsam and jetsam of the brain at rest. This one was loud and clear. She had been immersed in dirt, hands covered in it, digging, sifting, searching. She was looking for a part of herself, a vital part of her that was lost. It was hard to tell, so fleeting were the images, the feelings. Did she see it or feel it? She opened her eyes and shook her hands, lifted them to see if the dirt remained. They were unsullied.

Now with the sun shining, and her lace curtains fluttering in the early morning breeze it was becoming a distant memory, but the smell of the peat, the dirt, lingered. An innocent and innocuous circumstance brought a simple jar of dirt to her doorstep, to her mantel. Maddy knew there were things meant to be in their own time, at their own calling without the hand of humankind to guide or determine the when or the where of it. There was more in that jar of dirt than a pup getting into mischief. It seems she had been called to use her gift to find something or solve a deeper and much more ancient mystery. Her Gran's friend and the wee pup were just the messengers, of that she was certain, but the rest was a mystery yet. One asking to be seen to.

As much by nature as habit, Maddy was an early riser. You could get a lot done in the quiet of the early morning and it was always a treat to greet the sunrise with a cup of tea and warm bread just out of the oven. This morning, the loaves for the local store were cooling on the rack, a batch of savory scones as well, using up the last of the dried thyme in the cupboard before the new crop was dried and packaged.

The tide would be out now. With any luck, the kelp and seaweed stranded on the exposed rocks would be ready to gather and dry for a nice batch of sea mineral soap. Although the holidays were still months off, the soaps sold well last year, and Maddy was hoping to do multiple batches for the local stores. Handmade labels, with her Celtic M logo, artisan paper to wrap them in and a nice bit of raffia ribbon. All in all, special enough for a personal treat or a gift. The soap inside, with the minerals and seaweed, not only had a fresh sea scent, they were also soothing and healing for body and spirit.

The day was clear, bright, with a bit of a crisp breeze. She grabbed her shawl, her basket, straw hat and sunglasses. Gran's cottage was about a quarter mile from the seashore, a bit more if you went by the road, rather than through the fields and over the stone walls. The sheep in the fields paid her no mind as she rambled her way on the narrow, well-trodden path. The lichen-covered stones on the ancient walls were already warming from the sun.

Sometimes, when she laid her hand on them to clamber over, she could feel a thrumming and pulsing. The echo of the hands of ancient farmers, setting the stones one on top of the other, clearing the fields and marking their spaces. She was sure that some of the stones had been repurposed from even more ancient and mystical sites nearby. When she would touch one of these, she could feel an even deeper reverberation or essence rumble through, like distant thunder. The impenetrable veil of history usually kept these rumblings in the confines of the past, but Maddy knew that there were cracks, fissures and thin spots in the universe. Some cultures revered those landmarks, the standing stones, henges and solstice points, but she believed there were other places where the line blurred, just fleeting gaps in the shifts of the time-space continuum.

The sea was bright, sparkling and energetic, the waves slowly pushing back towards land, each cycle making a broader reach. Madeline easily spied the seaweed she looked for and carefully chose the shorter, younger strands. They would have the best scent and be the easiest to dry and crumble. She would leave the salt dried on them just as they came from the ocean. Her basket was soon full, and as she turned to go, took one look out to the sea. There, just before the horizon, there was something bobbing that caught her eye. Perhaps the head of a seal as it disappeared, then popped back up again.

Seals and Selkies, she thought. Legends abounded about these mystical creatures from the ocean. Seal when in the water, but human for a short time when out of the water. Selkies, if caught out of the water, could be held "captive," if their shed seal skin coat was hidden from them, therefore trapping them on land. Her skin tingled and her mind fell back into the archive of her dream and the frantic search for a covering, a skin. Suddenly, in her mind, she saw an image of a young, lithe woman in a rough woven cloak. There was desperation and darkness. There was no doubt that she was the one who'd been searching. She was the one seeking her lost skin, wanting desperately to go home. Blinking, the image was gone as quickly as it came. The waves rolled and danced, the sun sparkled on the droplets of salty splash. Out towards the horizon, the seal, if indeed there had been one, was gone.

Maddy pondered all the way back home. A Selkie without its skin couldn't return to the sea. He or she would be trapped on dry land. The woman in her dream had been digging, hoping for discovery and freedom. The dirt then was the key, and it must hold some clue, some essence, that would hopefully lead towards resolution. It was a reach for certain, but she'd start with a bit of research about the history and local legends around Ballrowan where her Gran's friend lived, perhaps she might find some hint there to make connections, or maybe not. It was a step, the first step. More, it *felt* like the right step.

After her local schooling, she had attended classes at the National University of Ireland in Galway. One of her favorite professors had been her history teacher, Ian Finegal. He would be the best one to advise her what books or resources to go to. As an authority on Irish history, he was accustomed to, and respected, the presence of the unexplained. The mysticism of standing stone cultures, the presence of otherworldly creatures, like Selkies, seemingly normal humans with paranormal traits, or wee folk, are all, literally, par for the course in Irish lore. To not believe in one is to not believe any of it. This would negate all of Irish History as far as Professor Finegal had been concerned. He liberally salted all his coursework with mysticism and Irish myth. They were intertwined and as complex as Celtic knotwork or Aran sweater patterns.

Once she got home from her seaside scavenging, there was no end to the projects and demands on her time. Wasn't that always the way. You've something on your mind to get to and so many other chores wiggle their way in with a chorus of 'me first, me first'.

A few days passed before she finally had a chance to dig up Professor Finegal's contact email and get in touch. She got a prompt reply, but not the one she had been hoping for. It seemed that her favorite professor had retired and taken himself off to New Zealand for a year. Part research on a book, part long overdue vacation. He said he would be happy to help as much as he could from such a distance, but suggested she email his replacement, Brennan O'Connor. *"Bren is as good as they come and will be a well-spring of information,"* he assured her in his response.

Although they'd never discussed it outright, Professor Finegal had been open to Maddy's questions and insights. He somehow understood, and therefore she had been more open, more transparent, with him than with any of her other acquaintances or Professors in University.

The thought of having to explain to anyone new how it came to her to be delving into this mystery was a bit daunting. The comfort was in Ian's trust and praise for his successor, which made her think that perhaps Professor O'Connor would be as open-minded and in sync with Ian's own take on Irish history and all its embellishments. If she was to follow the path inadvertently and literally put in

her hands, well, she would just have to be in touch
with the likes of Professor Brennan O'Connor and
see what came next.

THEN

The old woman had not lived alone for long. Moira's best friend and husband of twenty years had died the past winter. The work of keeping the fire stoked, feeding the animals and plugging leaks in the thatched roof had kept her busy, but now the weather had turned. The sun was out more than not. The animals were safely corralled in the field during the day, with plenty of new grass to eat. She missed her Hugh, missed him deeply and achingly. They had never had the pleasure of children, and although they had both come to terms with that long ago, she now wished for a family to turn to.

A walk would do her good. To get out beyond the walls of the little thatched hut and listen to the wind. The wind would have advice and stories to tell.

With a shawl tucked over her shoulders and under her arms and a small bundle of bread and fresh cheese tied onto her sash for later, she was ready to go. As was her habit, she checked the chickens and shook the latch on the old wooden gate where the cows and sheep grazed, before heading down the time-worn path to the sea.

Watching her steps carefully as she navigated the rocky slope to the beach, she did not at first notice the child. Once she had both feet on firmer, more level ground, she looked up and scanned the beach. There, not too far distant, was a child, a young girl, maybe six or seven years old. She was not always a good judge of these things, having never been a mother herself. The child was naked and alternately darted into the waves, teasing the tide, and then bending down to inspect some seaweed, or a shell perhaps. Whose child could this be? Moira could not think of any child this age from the village who would be left alone to frolic. They would be at their mother's side, weaving, cooking, or tending the farm animals, and most certainly fully clothed.

She approached quietly, but not so as to startle the girl. At one point, the child looked up and stood stock still, staring at Moira. Not with fear, the old woman could see, but with curiosity. Who was this fey creature? Shipwrecked? She had not heard of any, nor had there been a recent storm. Sprite? Specter? She certainly looked entirely flesh and blood. Moira put out a hand in greeting, as was the custom, to show she held no weapon. The girl was silent. "Do you speak, child?" Moira asked. The girl cocked her head to the side, as if trying to decipher her words. Maybe the poor thing was from beyond, and by some fantastical means had washed ashore here, practically in Moira's back yard. The old woman pointed to herself and said slowly and clearly, "Moira".

The girl did not respond. She merely stared at Moira for a few more seconds, then hunkered down to pick up a piece of seaweed and put it to her mouth.

"Oh, child, that won't be tasting good at all. Are you hungry then?" Moira untied the small bundle of food from her sash and reached in for a bit of the bread and cheese. When she looked up again, it could have been no longer than a minute, the girl was gone. There were only footprints washing away into the surf. The old woman searched the beach with her eyes, no sign of any life whatsoever. She knew she hadn't imagined the young girl —the footprints still barely visible, were proof. She looked out to sea, holding her hand above her eyes to get a better view.

She stared at the horizon for a long while, and then spied something that appeared to be a head. Was it her? The head turned to the side, and Moira could see it was naught but a seal. The lone seal stayed buoyant in the water and seemed to be staring right back at her. Could it be? She'd heard of such things, but to see it herself was another matter altogether.

Moira headed home, deep in thought. She was not deeply religious as such, but knew there were things beyond one small person's world. Knew there were forces out there that were to be respected and admired, appreciated even. Who made the spring come? Who could witness the birth of a lamb in the middle of a field in the middle of a storm and not appreciate the stronger forces of nature that embraced life, the constancy of it, the rhythm and the pattern.

There were things that happened for reasons unknown to mere mortals. Deep within her she understood that she would meet this young child again. She was part of a bigger plan, and would do her part to fulfill whatever destiny had in mind.

Was her heart lighter? No, not yet, but there was now hope and purpose where, after Hugh's passing, there had been despair and drudgery. Her future did not portend a monotonous daily life anymore. Her step was a bit lighter, and her afternoon chores accomplished with a bit more energy. Everyone, she thought, needs a purpose beyond themselves and their own small existence. Your everyday chores can feed your body, but it was hope that fed the soul.

The next morning, she woke, as always, just as the sun lightened the sky. After the animals were tended to, she had a small meal of cider, bread and cheese, and sat outside her door in the first rays of sun. She could smell the warmth rising from the earth and thatch around her. Sharp animal smells followed, along with the sound of bleats and snuffles beyond the gate.

Should she venture to the beach again today? Would the child be there? She waited quietly for a sign.

The Abbot from the Abbey in the village would insist she listen to his God, the one God that ruled all. She would never say it out loud, but she did not trust the Abbot. He had beady eyes, and would not look at you as he proclaimed and admonished. He was a bit too full of himself and not full enough of this God he believed in. Moira believed there was room for his God, and the spirits who reigned over life. One God could surely not be able to manage it all—the earth, the air, the water, the people, the animals. A bit of help was always welcome, whether in this world or the heavenly one. Moira kept very quiet about her opinions though. She'd witnessed the Abbot beating a young lad who had questioned him about believing in only one God.

One God, or many, they were all silent on this spring morning. Moira contemplated and pondered, but to no avail. Well, no sense wasting the day. There was always work to do around her small croft. Moira set about sweeping the dirt floor, setting to rights the pots and pans, and checking the grain stores for signs of rodents. Thoughts of the girl haunted her, though. Finally, she could wait no longer for direction from beyond. The pull, the need, was too strong and she set aside her homespun apron, grabbed her shawl, and headed out towards the beach.

THEN

The girl stepped softly, quickly, back into the cave by the sea. The rising tide lapped fiercely against the sides of the opening. Slipping once again into the skin she'd left behind, she felt her bones shift, her muscle memory form into the creature she'd been. An inexplicable miracle of metabolism, magic and myth. A shudder shook off the last of the earth-bound form as she slipped into the rising water along the cave's edge.

Saltwater streamed, shedding smoothly off her fur coat as she swam and dove, giddy with the speed and agility she regained. Hunger for fish as much as hunger for the familiar drove her deeper and deeper, farther and farther from shore.

And yet. There was something intriguing about the textures, the smells, the strangeness of the other place. To feel the grit of sand under foot. To have feet even, to stand, to stretch an arm out and wiggle fingers. All this and more, an unfathomable more.

Settling back into life with her colony of seals on the rocky shoals off the coast, she slept, swam, dove for fish and simply became one of the many. But she wasn't one of the many. She was one of a very rare few and she knew it. A deep knowing, deeper than the seas, deeper than the darkest night. A curiosity about the other became a siren call to be heeded.

And so she did. Swimming often and alone to the shore, to the hollow in the rocks, where she would shed her skin, stretch her arms, wriggle her toes. A place where the sand was dry and rough underfoot. Where she could chase the waves along the water's edge. The sun warmed her skin, so foreign at first with no fur to filter the harsh rays. She came to love the feel, the freedom.

Testing, tasting, touching and timing became her guides. Too long in the sun and her fair skin burned, too much handling of seaweed made for salt-crusted hands, saltier lips. What would delight for hours had time melting hour into hour and then she'd be scurrying to the cave at dusk to grope around for her skin. Her colony paid no attention to her comings and goings. Her experiences were beyond their ken. And so she too grew beyond their sphere, with no other like herself to share or compare. Solitude was filled with discovery, and then challenges, as she mastered the use of legs, arms, voice.

This solitude was not to last. One day a movement caught her eye and turning, she spied another on the beach. Previously it had only been the ones who soared in the skies, and an occasional four-legged, furred creature who shared her new domain. She knew not what any of them were called, but simply accepted them as other inhabitants. Paying them no mind, as they did likewise.

This one was different. Two legs and a covering, but not fur. The two-legged creature ventured closer and spoke. Not the guttural barks of her seal family, nor the squawks of the sky creatures but lilting and soft. "Mo-rah" it seemed to say.

Curious, she tried it. "Mo-rah."

The creature smiled and gestured. Treating it like the four-legged ones, she ignored it and went about her business, bending down to examine a piece of seaweed that washed ashore. Out of the corner of her eye, she noticed the two-legged stepping closer still and reaching into her covering. Prickles of caution danced up her spine. Slipping into the water and diving under a wave, she abandoned any further exploration.

Several turns of the sun and moon went by before curiosity won out over caution. She slipped quietly once again into the shallow cave at the water's edge.

NOW

Brennan looked at the stack of papers on his desk, to read, critique and grade. This was not a task he relished. He generally enjoyed teaching, heartened at the look on a student's face when they grasped the depth of it, the connections and the discovery. One or two students in the sixty plus he had each term would shine, and make it all worth the work of the others. But going through all those papers would be a slog. Even his star students could turn out disappointing work when it came to end of term papers.

Why not put it off just a wee bit longer? Surely a cup of coffee and a couple of biscuits would be just the thing before he went into battle.

With a steaming cup in hand and the small plate of shortbread set to one side of his laptop, he looked once again at the stack beckoning him. He switched on his laptop instead and thought to take a quick look at his email. The usual University junk mail, meeting reminders, pleas for help on various fundraisers, and a nice note from his former colleague and predecessor, Ian Finegal, which mentioned a woman, Madeline Murphy, who may be getting in touch with him for some advice on a project.

Great, he thought, *probably some old biddy with a passion for family history.* His time was already in short supply these days, but Ian was a good friend as well as his mentor. Brennan would make time for Ian's friend if she got in touch.

30 emails deleted, 5 emails responded to, and one last to go. He didn't recognize the sender and wondered if he should open it. You never knew these days. The last time his laptop had a virus, it took the IT department hours to clean it up. Thankfully he didn't lose any crucial work or correspondence, but it was a royal pain in the arse. Then he remembered Ian's friend. Madeline something? This was from "maddysmagic"... wasn't Maddy short for Madeline? Maybe Ian Finegal's

friend? Well, if she was emailing, maybe she wasn't so old after all, eh? Although, on the other hand, elder care facilities did a lot to help the older generation get connected and up to date with technology. He took a sip of his coffee, now gone cold, popped the last morsel of shortbread in his mouth and opened the email. It was indeed from Madeline.

Dear Professor Brennan,

My dear friend and former Professor, Ian Finegal, suggested that I be in touch with you about a particular project I am working on that requires some research direction and advice. I think it best to explain in person, if possible, and can arrange to meet you on campus at your convenience.

Thank you,
Madeline Murphy

Succinct, intriguing and mysterious. Brennan found himself replying immediately.

Dear Ms. Murphy,

It is the end of term, and my time is limited, but I would be able to meet with you for a short while on Friday, next. If it is agreeable to you, let's meet at The Harp and Whistle pub, at one o'clock.

Regards,
Prof. Brennan O'Connor

Succinct in return, with a built-in back door, in noting his limited time, to make his exit if needed. Brennan paused over the computer keyboard, then hit the send button. With a sigh, he lifted the first term paper off the stack, opened it up, put his feet up on his desk, leaned back and started to read.

Padrick, bartender and owner of The Harp and Whistle, looked up from the bar as the pub's large oaken door opened. A gust of wind, rain, and Brennan O'Connor came blasting in all at once. The door slammed shut and all was quiet for a moment. Bren threw back his anorak hood, shook the rain off, gave a quick nod to Paddy, with a raised finger to note one of his usual, and settled in at a table. It didn't take long for Sinead, the fetching young waitress, and one of his students, to bring him a Guinness.

"And, Professor, what'll it be—you're here for lunch as well, yeah? We've got Scotch eggs, lamb pasties and bangers and mash for specials." Her pen was poised on her tablet. Brennan wished she was as quick with the pen for her class notes.

"I'll just have a bowl of chowder—thanks, Sinead."

He was admittedly a bit early for his meeting with the mysterious Ms. Murphy. He'd brought along some reading and class notes, which he pulled out from his inner Anorak pocket and set on the table. Compared to many of his colleagues, he was young, and he wanted to give the impression of being dedicated and scholarly despite his age. He didn't consider himself vain, but did want to be taken seriously by Ian's elderly friend.

Bren looked up from his book and checked his watch-five minutes past one. Normally not a stickler for time, he was a bit fussed about the mysterious Ms. Murphy's tardiness. Well, he'd give her another twenty minutes. It was pouring buckets out, and if she was coming from some distance...come to think of it, he had no idea where she was coming from. He started to feel bad about not offering to meet her somewhere closer to her home. He wouldn't have wanted his grandmother out driving in this if she didn't have to. Then he remembered Ms. Murphy was the one who had offered to meet him on campus. Brennan went back to his reading. Each time the door blew open he looked up to see who the rain ushered in. Young Billy, a deck hand on the Aran Isles ferry, a few bedraggled tourists, Clyde, the local vet, a handful of students, but no sign of Ian's friend.

One more thump of the door opening, then quickly shutting to keep out the wild late spring weather. Bren looked up just in time to see the young woman who had come in push the hood of her cloak back and take stock of the occupants of the pub. Auburn curls haloed her head where they escaped the thick braid down her back. Fair skin, medium height, slender. He watched her step up to Paddy at the bar. Paddy nodded in Bren's direction in answer to her question. She turned then, and gray-blue eyes looked straight at him. Not a gray hair in sight, nor moth-eaten tweed. Brennan was recalculating quicker than his car's navigation system.

Maddy took a deep breath. No old, seasoned Professor here. Brennan O'Connor was young, good-looking and had her nerves tingling. Would he indeed be receptive to helping her? Well, as her Gran would say, "the butter only sets if you keep churning." She'd started the process, and if she wanted results she'd best keep going. Turning back to the barkeep, she asked for a Harp, and did they have a plowman's platter or something similar that could be brought around to the table? She wouldn't be able to eat it all, but she imagined the Professor could be enticed to share some.

"Yes, of course," answered Paddy. Padrick's years behind the bar had given him good ears, good eyes and tight lips. He would bet his best whiskey there was more here than met the eye.

"I'll have Sinead bring it by." He handed over the golden brew, expertly poured in a pint glass. She carefully took it and walked to the table where Professor O'Connor sat. She could see he'd been taken by surprise. He'd probably been expecting someone closer to her Gran's age with genealogy or ancient history on her mind. Well, he could be in for even bigger surprises.

"Professor O'Connor?" He nodded. "Madeline Murphy, but please call me Maddy." She set her glass down carefully across from him, unbuttoned her cloak, draped it over the back of the chair, set her satchel on the floor, then settled into a chair.

Brennan had to keep from staring. In jeans and a faded gray-blue sweater that made her eyes look as deep as the sea, she was a far cry from his moth-eaten image. Then she smiled and he was even more stunned, had to make an effort to focus on what she was saying.

"Sorry I'm late. It turns out that my Gran's old Rover has only one good wiper. It was all sunshine and gusts when I left home, but I should have known, Irish weather being what it is." And, she'd sensed the weather might be an issue with the Rover, whether common sense or uncommon sense, she kept quiet on that score. She'd spent a lot of her life keeping quiet. It was only in the last few years, after all that time with her open-minded and accepting Gran, that she was just beginning to be more confident and less worried about what others would think.

"No worries," Brennan replied. "As you can see, I brought along plenty of work to catch up on. Are you going to make it home okay, then, do you think?"

"The front seems to be blowing itself out, as it usually does and I should be fine. If it still looks threatening when I head back, I'll find a garage to see if they've what I need."

The two sat quietly for a moment then, Brennan idly stirring his chowder and coming to terms with the woman across the table, and Maddy wondering where to begin. Thankfully, Sinead came by just then with the platter and set it neatly between them. Sinead's eyes were taking it all in, and Brennan was sure there would be plenty of texting to her chums as soon as she was back behind the bar, about their professor and the lovely stranger at the pub.

"Please help yourself. I ordered more than I will eat, figuring you may be enticed to share or at the very least, I thought it would give us something to do if our meeting goes pear-shaped."

Brennan laughed. "I haven't heard that expression for years! I think my mum used to say that about gatherings with the rellies."

Quiet again, as they each set bread, cheese and sausage on their plates from the tray between them.

Oh dear, thought Maddy, *how to begin?*

"Thanks for meeting with me, Professor O'Connor. I know you are quite busy this time of year." *And how lame was that?* she thought. He was clearly waiting for her to explain her reason for meeting.

"Please, call me Bren, short for Brennan. I'm happy to help a friend of Ian's." He sipped his own brew as he watched her gather her thoughts.

She ran a finger around the rim of her glass, then looked straight at him.

"I'll not keep you and get right to it. I'm interested in any ancient legends about Selkies in this area. If you can think of any books, references, historic sites, or local stories, I would appreciate knowing of them." She took a sip of her Harp. "I don't need them now, but if you could email me any suggestions you may have..." she trailed off, wondering if she should explain more. This much could have been emailed to begin with but something had compelled her to ask to meet up with him. Trust was easier to gauge face to face —the eyes, the body language. Should she share with him more of the background of her quest, the why and the how of it?

"Selkies, eh?" The surprises kept coming. "That is an unusual topic to be delving into. Are you writing a book then?" Brennan's interest was definitely piqued. He had always been fascinated with the lines between myth, legend and historic fact. One led to the other and were twisted together like Celtic knotwork. As a young boy he read everything he could get his hands on that involved otherworldly creatures crossing into this world, and vice-versa. He believed there were places where the lines were thinner, almost transparent for those who could see, and those transparencies exposed or inspired creatures that defied earthly constraints.

A good teacher listens well. It is essential to any lesson plan, any class discussion. Bren had learned it tended to be true for life in general. He knew some people had more innate abilities to 'see' or anticipate what lay ahead. His own instinctual ability, he'd come to realize, was keener than some, but perhaps it was just that he paid attention. It is what made him a good teacher, tuning into his students' individual needs. His mum always said he had a knack to see through people, to understand them, but he didn't agree. He'd not paid heed to his instincts when it came to the disaster of his marriage which had ended in divorce several years ago. But he did pay heed now. He knew, could sense, there was more to her quest than simple research. He was intrigued.

As a history buff, he'd done his share of mudlarking along the Thames, or peat bog scavenging. He'd been on some archaeological digs as well, but they were tedious and time-consuming for parsimonious rewards. And too, good archaeological jobs were scarce, and the pay was barely livable at best. If he wanted to spend the day with dental tools, mucking around in someone's mouth was certainly more financially rewarding than mucking around in the dirt. He chose an avenue of history with job security and besides, he enjoyed teaching.

Still, discovering a glint in the mud, an odd shape, a potential treasure along with the detritus of earth, rock, plastic, and scrap, now there was fun and a rush of adrenaline. A bit of a poke with the trowel and you may just have a wee bit of history, valuable or not, in your hand. Maddy's interest in Selkies, and Maddy herself, if he was to be honest, was to him like that glint of hidden treasure—the promise of something more intriguing waiting to be discovered.

"No, not a book. But a mystery to be solved." Maddy took another sip and picked up a bite of cheese. "I don't have much to go on right now, more of a feeling, you know." She looked away at the other patrons in the pub, then looked back at the man across the table. He was not laughing at her or taking her request for information lightly. He nodded his head.

"I know just what you mean. Sometimes you get a whiff of something brewing, but you just can't put your finger on it. It's a bit ticklish."

The conversation turned casual then. They chatted about Ian Finegal's retirement, and Bren's teaching. He asked about her interest in Irish history, and where her interests led her now. She explained about her baking, and soaps and lotions, promoting traditional ingredients. Maddy touched briefly on living with her Gran, but did not go into the details.

Time passed all too quickly. Bren happened to notice the time on the big Guinness clock on the wall—already almost 2:45. He had a student meeting at 3:00 and needed to get going if he was to be at his office in time.

"Ach, I am sorry to say I've a student coming to my office at 3, so best be heading out. I'll do some scouting about for anything that may be useful for you. Shall I email or can I call you?" Clever chance to maybe get her phone number.

"Let me give you one of my business cards with both." She dug around in her satchel and pulled out a business card with a decorative Celtic M, then her name, Madeline Murphy, her email and her phone number.

Brennan wanted to pay for lunch, but Maddy insisted on paying. She'd asked for the meeting, for his help. "Next time it'll be on me," announced Bren. No room for argument either about the tab or the "next time."

They each gathered belongings, slipped on their coats, and with a nod of thanks to Paddy at the bar Bren opened the big oaken door for Maddy, then stepped out himself. The rain had quit, although the eaves were still dripping, and the sun was just starting to glint on the puddles in the street.

"I found parking around the corner just there." Maddy pointed up the street.

"I'm headed the other direction, so will say good-bye for now. It was a pleasure to meet you, Madeline Murphy." He liked how her name rolled so easily off his tongue. "I will be sure to be in touch soon."

"Same goes, and thank you for taking the time." Maddy didn't think twice about it, put her hand out and Bren took it in both of his rather than an impersonal shake.

Maddy's delicate hand was comfortable in his larger ones, and gave him a brief feeling of warmth. "Safe travels home, now."

He gently let go and she nodded, turned and walked away.

Bren watched her go for a brief minute. The hood of her cloak was down, and her auburn braid caught the sun with a glow of warmth. Did she shimmer, or was it just a flash off a rain puddle? He blinked, then saw her turn the corner, and she was gone. This was not the last he would see of her; he'd make sure of that. He pulled her card out of his pocket. Madeline Murphy—Murphy came from an old Gaelic word for sea-battler or sea warrior...hmmm...and she was looking for legends about Selkies, a mysterious sea creature—part seal, part human. For all her mild demeanor, he sensed a strong woman beneath that calm surface. But even a strong woman might need help. He looked forward to doing just that.

THEN

Moira found herself back at the beach more often than not over the next several weeks. Sometimes she would find nothing, sometimes faint images of footprints in the sand, and sometimes a seal out in the distance looking, she was sure, straight at her. She started bringing small gifts to leave just beyond the high tide mark. A necklace made of sinew cord and shells, a wooden bowl, made from a tree burl that Hugh had carved out. Then, one day, she started piling up small beach rocks into a wee cairn of sorts to keep her offerings a bit more protected. Each time she ventured onto what she now thought of as her spot of beach, she would check to see if her last gift was still there. Sometimes yes, but more often than not, no.

Did the Selkie girl have them? Had those pesky sea birds flown off with them?

Weeks had gone by, and Moira was beginning to wonder if she had simply imagined it all, a dream to comfort her loneliness. Summer was heading full on, and there were plenty more chores to do—milking, cheese making, a garden to tend, the sheep, cows and pigs to see to, and always the constant preparations for the winter ahead.

Still, she knew in her deepest being that there was a young Selkie girl out there. A young girl who would be back and need her someday.

The sheep would be shorn soon, and the wool carded and spun. The two young calves were ready for weaning, and the blacksmith's son would be here soon to trade work for one of the pigs. With all of this on her mind, Moira woke before the sun and decided to head to the beach just at sunrise, earlier than she usually ventured out.

The light was just beginning to shine on the tips of the waves as she stepped off the gorse-lined trail and on to the upper rock-strewn edge of the beach. Seaweed clung to the rocks where the tide had washed them ashore, and then abandoned them until the tide came back in to sweep the thick tangle of living strands back to the sea.

She noticed a slight movement up ahead. Could it be? Yes, there was the girl. As she stepped closer, she thought she could see the shell necklace around the child's slender neck.

When there was a new lamb, or skittish calf in the field, Moira had learned from Hugh, just sit still and wait. Curiosity or hunger or both will win out and they will come to you. Moira, itchy to get on with it as was more her nature, took a deep breath instead, and sat on a rock near the cairn. She pulled an oat cake out of her satchel, and made herself take slow small bites, quietly watching the young girl on the beach.

The girl glanced up, went about her ramblings, then looked up again. Moira sat and waited patiently. Surprisingly, she found it soothing to just sit and watch, a bit mesmerizing, actually.

She must have dozed off in the warmth of the sun. A screeching gull overhead brought her right back to the beach. Her backside was stiff and sore from sitting. How long? She had no idea. The beach was empty, with only the lazy tide-driven waves lapping endlessly back and forth.

Now, however, a renewed sense of purpose coursed through her. She resolved to be up early the next morning, and the next, for however long it took to gain the trust of this child. She had time. She had all the time it would take. Moira's legs were stiff and protested as she stood up. Rubbing her sore backside, she ambled her way back up the path. There would be plenty to catch up with back at her croft, keeping her busy until dark. Still, she did not regret one minute of her time on the beach. Greater forces than a mere human could fathom were at work here, she knew that, and she was a willing pawn in the scheme.

Moira witnessed a multitude of sunrises over the next month. At first the appearance of the child was sporadic—several days in a row, then a week with no sign. As the month wore on however, the older woman noted that the young girl, in her mind she had come to start calling her Ula, meaning "Jewel of the Sea," would show up on a more regular basis, and would always look down the beach toward Moira. Once she thought she saw the child nod, as if to acknowledge her existence.

It was a full moon, and the goats had gotten out in the middle of the night, wreaking havoc all over the yard. It took Moira hours to get them back in the pen and build a makeshift barrier she hoped would hold them until morning. She was lucky it was a bright moon, so getting them corralled was not as difficult as it could have been. Nonetheless, she found herself dragging the next morning, with plenty to do. It was later than usual for her daily trek to the beach.

Stepping out on to the pebbly sand, quickly scanning the beach, she sensed that the girl had come and gone. Out of habit, she made her way to her perch, near the cairn. There, on top of the jumble of rocks was a piece of sea-washed glass. Moira reached for it, turning it over and over. It was iridescent light blue, with some pitting and irregularities. She held it next to her heart. A gift from the child.

This was just the first of the small gifts that passed by way of the cairn over the next several weeks. A delicate dried starfish for Moira, a woolen shawl for the girl (Moira always worried the child was cold in the wee dawn hours on the beach), a salt-smoothed pottery shard with a small flower motif still visible on it, and in return, a simple linen shift (*she must be cold*, Moira thought, *without her fur*). They were each clearly aware of the presence of the other, one an aged, widowed, hardworking, simple peasant woman, the other a fey, mysterious changeling creature from the depths of the sea. An odd pair to be sure, but a match with a destiny.

Who knows how long this silent passing of gifts would have lasted. It came to an abrupt end one morning when Moira put a foot beyond the gorse bushes and onto the pebbly sand edge of the beach. She heard a soft wail. Suddenly, her arm was grabbed by the child. She was stunned at first, the flesh and blood of her, the truth of her, right there, tugging on her arm and making mewling noises. The reality quickly shifted to the young girl's frantic need to have Moira come with her down the beach. Moira patted the child's hand and nodded. "Go on then, show me what frets you so."

Her older legs could barely keep up with lithe young legs as they scrambled together among the seaweed, rocks and boulders along the beach's edge. The sun was just up, and the light had that misty ethereal feel about it. Finally, half out of breath and wondering how far they were going to go (would she be pulling her into the sea, then?), Ula let go of Moira's hand and ran ahead a bit, dropping down onto the wet ground next to a large seal. A big brown eye blinked and whiskers twitched, the girl smoothed the fur on the creature's head. The poor thing was in great trouble. It was impossibly tangled up in a flaxen and sisal fishing net and breathing heavily from what must have been hours of exertion trying to disentangle itself, and more likely than not, making matters much worse. Clearly a full-grown animal that was too large for young Ula to help on her own.

She carefully bent down on her creaking knees and laid a hand on the soft fur. "I will help you, shh, shh, I will do no harm," she crooned softly. While she spoke quietly and soothingly, her hands roamed the netting to find a hold where she could begin to work the salt-stiff fibrous strands away from the seal's body. She knew time was of the essence if she was to save the seal's life. The trust Ula had placed in her gave her the confidence and strength to ply the cords firmly, continuously and methodically, loosening, twisting, motioning for Ula to help her roll the furry body this way and that as the netting was slowly untangled.

NOW

Maddy carefully drove the Rover through the hedge opening and down the bumpy puddle-strewn lane that led to the cottage she shared with her Gran. She had stopped on the way home for fish, carrots, and cream to make a chowder. As she got out and turned to grab her satchel and basket of purchases, her Gran came out to meet her. "Well, then, how did ye do with your new professor?"

Maddy looked up to see the spritely older woman wiping her hands on a linen towel and smiling broadly. Her Gran seemed ageless, but Maddy knew the hands of time did not stand still for anyone. A little more stooped, a little slower in the mornings and evenings, a little bit of a wistful far-off look once in a while—a strong woman still, but bit by bit, fading.

"Ah, now, wouldn't you really be wanting to know if he was young, handsome, and unmarried?" Maddy tossed back with a flip of her braid and a grin.

"Well, now that you mention it..." said her Gran.

"I'll not have you making any assumptions, or plans for my future, but yes, he's all three."

"Saints be praised," whispered the older woman, with her eyes lifted skyward.

"Now, Gran, he may have someone already, and I didn't say I was interested, anyway."

"I worry about what will happen to ye when I am gone, love, so let an old woman have her dreams." With that being said, she hooked her arm through Maddy's and walked back to the house with her. Annie Donahue didn't have the sight, like her granddaughter, but she did know when to keep her own counsel. Where there was potential there was hope, and with a bit of human and divine intervention (a bit of prayerful instruction to the Lord wouldn't hurt), well, you never knew.

Brennan O'Connor had drifted through his student meeting on auto pilot. His thoughts kept shifting to an enchanting woman with a mystery to solve. He sat at his desk that evening, with a coal fire crackling in the shallow fireplace to fend off the damp and chill of late spring, his desk lamp glowing next to his laptop with his class notes open and waiting.

He'd propped Maddy's card right up against the Waterford crystal pen holder his ex-wife, Christine, had given him when he got his undergraduate degree over 8 years ago. He'd given her a diamond engagement ring.

They'd met as undergraduates at Trinity. He had a family name, but not piles of money, she had the piles of money but not the historic family credentials. His family accepted his choice with grace that came from good breeding and manners, but they never really took to her, he could see that now.

He had been young, and charmed by her attentions. Glamorous, wealthy, comfortable in a world his family hadn't been a part of for generations. New money, from hedge fund trades and real estate had seen Christine growing up in privilege, but not quite accepted by the old guard blue bloods. They married just after graduation, then lived simply, by her standards, while they both went on to graduate work. She in International Economics, he in Irish History.

It didn't take long for Christine to realize that he was not interested in attending social events that would heighten their status, he was comfortable with who he was, and who he socialized with. He would rather go to the pub with his pickup soccer mates than a fancy affair. She got tired of appearing solo at many of the season's gala society events and having at the ready a plausible excuse for his absence. She demeaned his choice of friends, then cajoled, pleaded, and whined for him to elevate his standards. There came a time when she stopped buying him any gifts, lavish or otherwise, and she finally stopped paying for any of their married expenses. Thank goodness she hadn't been in favor of having children right away. Too much fuss and bother, and her figure would have suffered, she'd said. At one point he finally moved into the guest bedroom.

When he raised his head from his studies long enough to notice a gossip rag on a pub table with a photo of Christine arm-in-arm with a young Italian count, he knew it was time to pull the plug. He'd known it for a while, truth be told, but was frankly too absorbed in teaching and getting his graduate degree and happy to have space to breathe when Christine was occupied with her own pursuits to do anything about the sham of a marriage. He knew his family tried to talk to him during that time about the obvious cracks. He would just nod, take a swig of stout, and say, "Yeah, we're working on it." Uh huh... like anyone believed that.

A short divorce and a hefty payout got him free. He took advantage of what was left of his share of a small family trust to go from the divorce to burying his head in his PhD studies. He'd lost track of Christine. Once in a while he would notice her photo in the society sections of the Dublin Times or London papers, but he had no lingering anger or angst. They had both been equally at fault, young and foolish. He was content with his life now. He hoped she had found the same.

He'd had some short-lived relationships, and female friends galore, but no serious sparks, until now. Maddy lingered, like fine wine. He was looking forward to another taste of that particular vintage. Selkies, eh? Well, he'd finish up his class notes and start checking a few leads he had in mind.

NOW

Maddy's thoughts wandered while she was baking, picking herbs, and helping her Gran, to a certain young professor of Irish history. She knew he was busy this time of year with exams, final papers, and student projects. He'd be in touch, of that she was certain. As she examined her impression of him, with distance and time on her side, she felt he was going to be someone she could trust, someone who would embrace and support her gift, as her Gran had. She smiled at the thought of the young professor meeting her Gran—now wouldn't that be a fine time for all.

Spring was in full bloom, the fields a legendary deep green the Irish Isles were justly famous for, the early bulbs and flowers bursting, the air fresh and windswept. Maddy had just been given a job of putting together 24 gift baskets for a very posh baby shower. One of her Gran's friends from church was the mother-in-law, her son married to the Lord Mayor's daughter, and they had wanted something unique with a touch of what her Gran had promised to be 'her special gift'. Now, what did Gran mean by that? Her mystical insights or her creative ones? She would, of course, put both into her creations for the celebration of the new child. She idly wondered if they knew it was going to be a girl.

The kitchen table was overflowing with delicately woven sea grass baskets, ribbons, daffodils and daisies for new beginnings, ferns for youth, rosemary for healing, lavender & mint tea for ease of sleep and happiness and of course, a bit of baby's breath. Maddy tucked small packets of the tea, along with delicate soaps, flower and fern sprays, and a small silver charm provided by the parents, into a pleasing arrangement in each basket. Flowers in one hand, ribbons the other, baskets in all stages, and the phone rang. *Isn't that always the way?* thought Maddy, *it's probably one of those marketing blokes wanting to offer a good deal on car insurance.* She let Gran get it in the other room but would keep an ear out. She could hear her chatting up the person on the other end. *Oh saints be, please don't talk her into a new telly, or donating to some charity no one has ever heard of.* Maddy knew her Gran was not easily taken in, but still, these fellas could be awfully persistent and persuasive.

Just then, she walked in with the phone held out to Maddy. "It's your nice professor fella, calling to see if you can meet up with him."

Maddy took a breath…well, hadn't she been waiting for him to call or email? Her heart kicked up into a rapid beat as she wiped her damp hands, then reached for the phone. Another deep breath, "Hello Professor O'Connor."

"Brennan, or better yet, just Bren, please—Professor O'Connor is some old fusty guy in tweeds and scuffed brogues."

"Okay, Bren it is then."

"I've a few places I'd like to show you that may help your research, not far from Galway. If there is a time that works best for you, I thought we could meet again at the pub and go together from there." There, it was said. Brennan didn't know why he was nervous as a schoolboy.

He'd remembered a medieval manuscript that had marginalia with depictions of a seal-child among other telling graphics. The manuscript itself was purported to be connected with an Abbey, now just ruins, in Kilneamh. He'd taken some time to track down information about it just to confirm his recollection. The area was lousy with ruins, standing stones and history. It wasn't conclusive, but a start. Then he agonized over asking her to join him to do some exploring. He could have simply emailed the information and let her go herself. That, he realized, however, was never an option. He was not one to pass up a mystery, especially one involving mystical creatures, and he was certainly not going to pass up an opportunity to see Maddy again.

"Okay, but I've a few projects to finish up by the end of this week. What about Sunday, or would a day next week be better? Do you still have students and classes?"

"Classes are finishing up. I've a few student reviews and some faculty meetings, but nothing this weekend. Let's aim for Sunday. Can you meet me around noon at the pub, then? Dress comfortable and casual, we may be taking a hike after."

"Okay, yes, that would be fine. I'll see you then."

"I look forward to it, Maddy."

Maddy looked at the phone receiver for a few seconds. That simple—a lead, a time, another step in a journey that had been beckoning from the mantel for months.

THEN

Being a widow was not an easy life. On the one hand, it did give her the rare opportunity to claim property, but if the land was choice, there were plenty of widowers who would look covetously upon it and find a way by friend or foul to have it for their own. Moira and Hugh had fortunately made a mark in their small community of crofters and tradesmen, and Moira was respected as a hardworking, honest and Christian soul. This respect gave her some modicum of protection from marauders, thieves or swindlers.

Small communities being what they are, though, news spreads. Moira's regular trips to the beach did not go unnoticed. A young lad trailing a stray lamb even came back with word of an unknown young girl seen on the beach with Moira.

Moira became aware of the whispering, and understood that some explanation would need to be made and the rumors set straight before they got out of hand. A widowed single woman with a croft of her own was already an oddity. Adding unusual behavior and a mysterious child into the mix could spell a disaster that could set her world, and perhaps Ula's as well, tumbling.

Her closest neighbors, and friends, were a young couple, Gwain and Esthwyn. Gwain had taken over his father's croft. They had been blessed with several children, one boy and the rest girls. One of the girls, Moira guessed, was about Ula's age. Who better to ask, and who better to help build the foundation of a plausible story for Ula's presence. Moira put together a basket of bread, cheese, and some herb tea, as Esthwyn was with child again, to take as a gift in exchange for some advice.

The day was fine, and she finished her chores in good time. Esthwyn, she knew, did laundry as often as not on a good sunny day, so she felt sure she would find her at home. A full basket tucked under her arm, she started up the road towards the young family's croft. Up the hill, around the bend, just past the standing stone where Moira stopped and crossed herself for piety and luck, she could see a wisp of smoke trailing up from where the farm was nestled. As she neared, she spied their oldest girl, Elyn, stirring the big iron pot with the wash, a younger sister, Brighid, next to her dipping the clothing in cooler water and wringing the water out, then on to the youngest, Margreta, who, one linen garment at a time, stood up on a log end and hung the wet clothing over the sisal rope strung between the hut and the barn. Esthwyn was supervising while scraping a hide on a stretcher for parchment, her belly large with their 5th child.

The quality of Esthwyn's parchment was well known in the region. The scraped and treated hides would provide the Monastery with material for the monks to write their holy texts on. It was also a valuable commodity for the family for taxes and tithes.

"Hello the house," sang out Moira. Esthwyn and the girls looked up, the oldest giving a wash reddened hand wave of acknowledgement, and Esthwyn setting down her scraper to walk towards the gate.

"Moira, you are welcome." The young woman opened the gate, and the older woman stepped through to the dirt yard, ringed with herbs, stone walkways and of course the tripod holding the wash pot over the fire in the middle of it all. Chickens scurried underfoot, pecking for bugs and bits, and a cow bellowed from the far thatched barn, answered by the baaaa of a sheep.

"I don't mean to disturb your work, for even with such fine help, I know 'tis more than a full-time business to keep croft and family going."

"Yes, and Gwain is out fishing today with Alfred, but we can take a bit of time to visit if you'd like. The girls are almost done with the washing, and I am ready to take a rest. My back is bothering much of late as the babe is eager to be out. I am sure 'twill be a boy—he is so demanding, already," replied Esthwyn, with a tired smile, while stretching and rubbing her sore lower back.

"I've brought you some bread and cheese, and some herb tea I think you will find soothing."

"Ah, how kind. I will have one of the lasses put the kettle on." With that she signaled to Brighid, and handed her a pot for water, to set on the coals under the tripod.

The two women sat on the bench, by the door, in the sun, while the girls set the tea to steep, and placed chunks of bread and cheese on a linen cloth.

After catching up on village news, exclaiming over how the girls had grown, and remarking on the weather, it was time to get down to business.

Moira took a breath. "I've the need to ask for some advice, Esthwyn, if I may."

Esthwyn looked surprised, but nodded.

"You may have heard," (she was sure Esthwyn had, how could she not?), "of a young girl I have befriended. I believe her to be from a shipwreck, as she just appeared one day on the beach beyond the cliffs. I think she has managed to make a crude home among the caves just below the cliffs. She does not speak, and was quite hesitant at first, but I have been able to get her to wear some modest clothing, and I bring her food. She needs a true home, and I feel that God has put her in my path to take care of her and bless an old childless widow in her shadow years." She hesitated. Like tea, the words needed to steep to be of any real good.

"She may be about the age of your Elyn, although I am not the best judge of these things," she admitted. "I just wish to know how best to proceed. How best to get her to settle in with me, rather than a desolate cave. I fear for her well-being and her soul."

Esthwyn looked down at her hands holding her rough clay mug of tea. She looked back up at Moira. "This is truly a sign from God, and if God wills, you will find a way. Steering children on a righteous and honest path is not easy, even when they are your own from birth." The young mother looked skyward, as if the heavens would provide some inspiration or answer.

"Trust is important, and nourishing her soul as well as her body may be key in building that trust. Has she not yet come to your croft, or seen your farm animals? Perhaps there is a way to entice her? I find that curiosity and food are often welcome temptations for accomplishing unwelcome chores."

Moira considered the possibilities. She would not force the child to do anything that she would not offer by free will. Well, as Esthwyn had pointed out, if God wills it to be there will be a way.

The two women sat quietly together, each deep in her own thoughts, and watching the young girls finish the laundry, chase the chickens, look for eggs and make pictures in the dirt with sticks.

The sun slipped behind a cloud, and it seemed to break the spell. It was well past time to get back to the calls of daily life. Moira set her hand on the younger woman's arm. "Let me know if you need me when the babe comes."

"Thank you Moira, by the Gods." She crossed herself to emphasize her Christian faith over her still deep-rooted faith in multiple Gods. "It will be an easy birth, but I'll send Elyn to you if otherwise."

Moira slipped her basket, now weighted with fresh eggs the girls had found, over her arm and slowly walked back. Although she hadn't found ready answers, she felt that Esthwyn was right, the direction would come if she listened and heeded.

THEN

Word of the young girl on the beach had indeed spread. Who did she belong to? Where had she come from? The Abbot of the Monastery of Kilneamh heard these whispers and more. He was a pious man, and considered himself a true chosen instrument for Rome and God. He was meticulous and precise, but he was not, by nature, kind, nor broad-minded. He was not known for having a generous nature, nor a soft soothing manner. He simply had neither. Had been offered neither as a child.

How far he'd come from the wretched creature he'd been. Dropped off at night like a stray. A rag of a boy for the monks to sweep up or discard of as they pleased. No name, no age, no past. Left for the monks to bury if he died, to do as they wished with if by the saints he lived to see another day. He lived, if you could call it living, he thought now. His hands folded over a corpulent belly, a full belly, in front of a warm fire. He closed his eyes, measured the distance of his memory, back to when he'd worked and watched, unnoticed, as he scrubbed floors, stoked fires, lugged water. He was impugned to suffer in the name of service to a higher power. That higher power, he saw, wasn't heavenly, nor spiritual. As he'd seen with his own eyes that those with power had food and fire, wine, women and riches. Abbots, Bishops, even the Pope, he supposed, although he'd never seen His Holiness.

He aspired, conspired, even as he perspired in the name of that higher power, in the name of all that was holy and righteous. One day he would command, one day others would do his bidding. One day he would have power and gold, food and fire, and he thought as he stroked his lap, women, forbidden fruit, to be plucked and savored in the dark.

He sat back comfortably in his chair, legs extended towards the fire, a fine wine in his hand.

Yes, God had presented him with a mission, to cleanse the peasant class of their earthy natures, elevate their devotion and be rewarded in the afterlife. For these efforts, he believed he deserved to be rewarded in his current life. He was, after all, performing God's will, and given his status was entitled to reap whatever benefits he saw fit. No one questioned him, he made sure of that. But he'd been bored lately, and news of this strange girl intrigued him, piqued his interest. He took a sip of his wine. Yes, he would watch and plan.

And so it was that on fine days, more often than not, the Abbot wandered toward the cliff road and walked the fields along the coast. These supposed solitary contemplations with God, as he described his outings to the monks under his tutelage, were, in truth, in hopes of spying the mysterious young girl. A glimpse of her would cement his plans for her future. He was certain she was sent for him, *to him*, and the peasant woman was just the messenger, the avenue of God's doing to present this untouched and unearthly child for his tutoring and care.

One morning, earlier than his usual outings, his efforts were rewarded by a sighting of her walking the beach with the old woman. The sun was bright and glinting off the waves. He dared not try to get any closer to the edge of the cliff, nor take the time to find a way down to the beach. Indeed, why should his efforts be so strenuous when he was sure with patience he could find a way for her to come to him. What he could see showed a lithe body, long flowing hair, and natural graceful agility. He did not need to see her close up to know he wanted her. Of course, he told himself, so he could guide her, restrain her fey nature and mold her mind to servitude to God. To lead a pious productive life, as all women were instructed, by the Lord himself.

On his way back to the Monastery, he ducked into a small cavern, under old standing stones, just a short path off the road. It had been used for seasonal rituals. When he was new to his elevated position, he had broken up a gathering there one spring with torches and armed guards. The few who were captured were strongly encouraged, by uncomfortable, if not fatal means, to repent their old ways and embrace one God. As far as he knew, and he had spies who would tell him otherwise, the cavern had not been used again for such unholy purposes.

He furtively searched the hills around. Green rolling fields, stone walls, a view of the village in the valley, but no-one to see him tuck down the path and into the cavern. It was dank, musty, the air smelled of mystery and ancient rhythms. A natural stone gap in the top allowed the light in. This light was once celebrated and worshipped. The Abbot was not there for the light, but for the dark, the hidden. He took his heavy jeweled gold cross and chain off his neck, kissed the ruby at the center, and then tucked it in his pocket. The journey he was about to take was on the road with the devil himself. He knew this but could not stop himself. At the very least, he would not be chained by God while he travelled this path. He then settled onto a stone bench and let his vision of the young girl and his hands take over. When he was done, and his mind and body emptied, he cleaned his hands, wiping them on the damp moss and stone, then stood, took the cross out of his pocket, kissed it once again, and placed it over his head to settle around his neck, its opulent weight nestled on his chest. He crossed himself, conveniently absolving himself of sin, took a breath and stepped back out into the sunshine.

NOW

Brennan had been watching the calendar and the clock as well. Sunday could not come soon enough now that he had made the leap of faith that any burgeoning relationship requires. He rushed through his students' final papers, final exams and any advisory duties. The stack of reference books was piled on his nightstand along with pages of notes on Selkie myths, some far-fetched and far-afield, and some he discovered ran a bit closer to home.

Like the one he'd remembered and spurred him to set up his date with Maddy. He'd tracked down a Medieval manuscript with relevant marginalia. These small and sometimes historically informative drawings on the side of the religious texts gave clues to life behind the scenes, or were subtexts to meaning. Only nobles of great wealth or someone in the church would have had the skill to read and write and the funds to pay for parchment or leather binding. Journals with written notations of daily life were scarce. Books were limited to religious texts or so-called books of hours, and these would have been specially commissioned by and written for a Noble family. Any gleaning of daily life or notable events were carefully mined nuggets that historians found between the lines of these texts and from the naive yet elaborate drawings within them. Meant as 'text' for the illiterate populace of the time, the drawings served as a valuable record of everyday life, allegories, myth, cautionary tales or flights of fancy.

Stories and myths about Selkies on the Irish shores were fanciful and plentiful, but when you started to pick them apart most were fashioned out of whole cloth and not based on verifiable facts or even recognizable places. Stories overlapped, contradicted themselves and were a tangle he painstakingly picked apart. Between vague references in historical texts and combing through Medieval manuscript marginalia, he'd finally found the thread he'd been looking for. One that held and led to another, which led to another, all pointing towards ancient stone structures and monastery ruins near Ballrowan. This is where he was planning to take the delightful Miss Madeline Murphy. First stop would be the pub to tell her what he found out. Then, if the weather permitted, perhaps a trip to the stone structures or the Monastery ruins. Even if the thread was a dead end, it was a start, and would show Maddy his faith in her and the mystery she was trying to solve.

He had it all planned out. Keep it simple and dazzle Maddy over lunch and beer at the pub with his insightful and brilliant research.

It was a terrific plan until he chatted on the phone with his sister Erin.

"Oh, Bren, you can't just flash your old books in her face at the pub for God's sake. That has dodgy old professor written all over it."

"Well, I am a dodgy old professor," Bren shot back.

"Hmm, well, I'll give you the dodgy bit maybe, but not the old. Get the pub to pack a lunch, have a picnic if it's nice. Some place with a view."

"What if it rains, then what, soggy bread, and soggier date."

"Now, don't be an eejit—use the brain I know is in there somewhere. You always have a plan B. A picnic in the Rover if you must—but park it somewhere with a view."

As soon as he hung up with his sister, Bren called the pub and had no trouble arranging to pick up a basket ready to go. He pushed 'end call' on his mobile, sat back and put his feet up. He had to admit Erin had a good suggestion. He felt pretty confident things would fall into place without a hitch.

"Now, Gran, if you're not feeling well, I'll not go." Maddy held her Gran's hand and was not so subtly feeling her pulse and her strength.

"Nonsense, child. I will be right as rain in no time. I'm sure 'tis just a touch of the bug. Father Sean had a bit of the sniffle at Mass yesterday morning and likely I've got it now too." The older woman pulled her hand out from under the lap blanket and patted the top of Maddy's hand. "You go and have a good time with yer young fella. It does my heart good to see you out and about a bit."

"All right then, but I've written my mobile number on a paper next to the phone. You'll not hesitate to call if you need to." It was a statement, not a question. Gran was silent for a few seconds. "Promise me?" Maddy looked her straight in the eye. Her Gran had always said a promise was a promise, and not to be taken lightly or broken.

"I promise, but don't you go worrying ta yourself about me. Now, do ye promise?"

She had her there—a promise is a promise and not to be taken lightly or broken.

Maddy smiled and hugged her. "I promise." She hoped Gran couldn't see that she'd crossed her fingers behind her back.

The day was fine, in contrast to the last time she had driven to Galway. She found a parking spot along the street, not far from the pub where Brennan was waiting outside. He hadn't seen her yet and she had the luxury of just watching him for a few minutes. Clearly a well-worn and well-loved denim jacket, soft gray tee shirt, jeans and sensible hiking boots. He looked a sight. She could almost imagine him in one of those fancy rugged-wear catalogs. He was leaning against the old stone front of the pub, one leg bent up against the wall, a basket on the ground next to him, concentrating on a paperback book held open in his hands. His dark hair blew a bit in the breeze. It was on the longish side—a hint of a curl over his collar, and a bit tucked behind his ear.

She sighed and opened the car door. Time to take the next step. She slung her satchel over her head and shoulder, locked the car, tucked the keys in her bag and headed for the pub.

He looked up when he heard a car door shut with a thunk. Yep, that would be an old Rover for sure. There was Maddy herself, as intriguing as he remembered. He bent over to tuck the book in the basket, grabbed it up and turned to face her.

"I thought we'd take advantage of a rare sunny day and have a bit of an outing, if that suits you. I've had Padrick pack us a lunch to bring along."

"Aye, its fine, but if it's a ways, I'll need to follow you in my car. Gran wasn't feeling well this morning, and I've made her promise to be in touch if she needs me to come home."

"I'm sorry she's ailing." He laid a hand on her arm.

"Just a touch of a bug she says she probably got from Father Sean at church and nothing to fret about, but I do worry a bit." She looked up at him with a grin. "She's a strong one though and not about to let a sniffle or two have her lifting an oar out of the water for long. Still, if we need to drive I'd feel better about separate cars, just in case."

Bren was a bit disappointed about this slight shift in his 'perfect' date plans, but it was a minor hiccup in the scheme of things. His natural good nature took over quickly. She was still here, he could still dazzle her with his brilliant research, and she was still going to get to hear his great find on her behalf.

"Well, then, I'll just go get my car—it's parked around the corner. Wait at yours and I'll meet you."

He pulled up alongside where Maddy was waiting. She nodded and signaled he should go on ahead. He then headed up the road slowly, allowing her time to slip in behind him.

The weather could not have been better. As usual along the coast, the breeze was a constant companion, but the skies were deep blue, the sun bright. Maddy had no trouble following as Bren was a considerate guide, keeping a moderate speed and distance ahead of her, and making sure she was still behind him after a turn or a curve in the road.

He finally put his signal on and pulled into an open spot in a field. The field rambled downward and was crisscrossed with ancient stone walls, all the way to the cliff edge. The ocean sparkled just beyond, the waves were a bounty of jewels tumbling to shore. Maddy parked carefully in the field next to him. Two Rovers, one old and a bit battered, the other newer, flashier. Even with the differences, they looked like they belonged side by side. It was a fleeting impression that flashed through Maddy's mind before Brennan came up next to her with the basket in his hand, his other stretched out for her to take.

She took it and let him lead her through a break in a stone wall to the other side. The stone wall was at their backs, protecting them from the breezes, and there was a sliver of the ocean view in front. It was a perfect setting for their picnic.

Brennan felt an odd buzz as he took hold of Maddy's hand to lead her to the spot he had scoped out a few days before. When he let go to set the basket down, he realized it was still warm and tingly. How odd, maybe he had a reaction to some lotion she used. It had never happened before, but they put so much odd organic this and that in stuff anymore who knew? He rubbed his hands together and then gave it no more thought.

Maddy had felt it too, something, a warning? A recognition? And wondered if Bren would say something. She watched him carefully as he glanced at his hand after he let go, staring at it for a few seconds with puzzlement. She braced herself to provide some sort of response, although she wasn't sure what that response would or could be. Then, he shook his head and went about spreading a car boot blanket on the grass, and with a sweep of his hand invited her to sit.

"Bren, it's a fine spot for lunch." Madeline slipped her shoes off, sat down on the edge of the blanket and tucked her feet under her.

"You can actually thank my little sister, Erin. When I mentioned our meeting, she suggested I would have dodgy old professor stamped on my head if I dazzled you with my research and books at the pub. 'A picnic,' she says bold as brass, 'now there's the thing'. In my younger years I wouldn't have listened quite so keenly, but I've learned that she sometimes has the right of it after all."

Bren popped the tops off of two bottles of Guinness, handing one over.

Maddy took her bottle of stout and raised it. "Here's to Erin then, and to her big brother learning to pay attention." She grinned as she lifted her bottle towards him.

They clinked bottles together and each took a swallow, the rich mellow brew sliding smoothly down their throats.

"Let's see what Padrick packed, shall we?" Bren said as he set his bottle down and started rummaging around in the basket, opening packages and plastic tubs, plates and cutlery.

Maddy soon joined in, as the basket seemed to be bottomless. Cheeses, olives, sausages, nice crusty bread, French bean salad, shortbread biscuits and raspberries.

"Are you sure you told him it would just be the two of us then?" Maddy's eyes were full of the quantity of food that was strewn on practically every square inch of the blanket.

"I did tell him to pack us a hearty lunch," said Bren as he piled sausage and cheese on a slice of bread.

"He did that and more. Was he hoping, then, that a wee bit of drink and a full belly would make me swoon at your professorial brilliance?" Maddy quipped back.

"Na, I can impress ye all on my own, without the help of the stout and the food." Bren proceeded to take a big bite of his haphazardly constructed sandwich.

Maddy was a bit tidier about it all, setting a wedge of cheese on a thick slice of bread, and placing a few raspberries on the top. The tart sweet of the raspberries mingled with the smokey sharpness of the cheese, in perfect harmony. She closed her eyes and savored the taste, savored the weather and the day itself. She hadn't dared, or had much opportunity, truth be told, to go out on a real date. She liked Bren, it was as simple as that. Felt relaxed and comfortable in his presence. She was beginning to believe he was someone she could trust.

They sat in companionable silence, enjoying the bounty of the basket, and each other's company. Words did not seem necessary. It was enough to share the moment.

They eventually got around to chatting about this and that—his work, her work. She told him about making the baby shower baskets. He talked about his students and summer classes coming up. It was easy and natural. Madeline began to let down her guard, went ahead and spoke what was on her mind without too much thought ahead of time.

The lunch was soon just mostly empty containers and crumbs on the boot blanket. The bottles of Guinness empty. Had they really eaten it all? She was astonished. Certainly, with his size he'd eaten more than she, but still, she'd managed her share.

NOW

Bren started to pack the basket up, tucking all the trash into one container. Madeline appreciated his thoughtfulness, ensuring no human intrusion would be left behind in this idyllic spot.

"While we're here, I've an interesting site to show you, if you're up for a short hike," said Bren as he stood and brushed the crumbs off his lap. "It's something I've known about but never been to."

"Sure," said Maddy and stood, grabbing one side of the boot blanket, shook it out and folded it up.

"There's some standing stones just yonder, and the remains of a cavern. I came across references to it when I was doing some research on myths and legends in the area. It's said it was used for rituals during solstice, until round about the 13th century, an Abbot from Kilneamh Abbey rather violently disapproved and forbade the practice, at least according to some legends, or it may have just fallen into disuse and disrepair on its own."

He kept talking as they put the trappings of their picnic into his Rover. "I found some old marginalia that implies the Abbey and these standing stones may have connections you'd be interested in." Bren then turned around, shading his eyes, and nodded towards the East. "I think it's easiest to head over that way."

Stepping back through the gap in the stone wall, and down a barely visible path, Bren took the lead holding her hand, then letting go when the path was only wide enough for one at a time. Maddy stayed right behind.

"Ah, just here I think," said Bren, as he turned through some heavy overgrowth. The landscape made a dramatic change beyond the scrub brush. The topsoil had been worn right down to rock ledge in most places, with tufts of grassy spots clinging on to whatever bits of soil were hidden from winds and time. Maddy could see the ancient bones of a structure. A large slanting flat rock balanced atop two others and sloped into a natural rise in the land, creating a cavernous opening. The pillar stones were tilting now, but still vertical enough that Maddy was able to envision them in their youth, their strength. How did the ancient ones ever move them into place? Still, after all this time she could feel the rhythm, the heartbeat of the universe around them. How did they know, all those years ago, where the veil was the thinnest? She supposed without all the noise, internal and external of modern culture, one would be more in tune with the subtle ebb and flow of time and nature. Now we paid yoga instructors and therapists to help you center and find that core. It is still here, has been here all along. It is simply that humankind has forgotten how to look and listen.

Brennan watched Madeline stop and stand still, as if listening to the field in front of them. She had a look of concentration he found fascinating, as if she was absorbing the very history of the rocks and earth underfoot. Then she looked up and smiled at him, walking on to catch up with him.

With such an uneven surface, they each picked their own way through the rock-strewn field. Madeline agilely clambered over juts of stone and made it to the edge of the structure just ahead of Brennan. She casually reached out to touch it.

It was a jolt. It was a thunderclap. It shook her to her core. She stumbled back a step and wrapped her arms around herself, as if they would provide protection from an attack. It was an attack of sorts, she thought vaguely, then all thought was gone. Darkness, pure evil started pulling her down, down, and she resisted as best she could. Visions came and went, in a chaotic and macabre dance, and she could catch only a few clearly. An Abbot, or was it a monk? Stone, cold, dark, damp, lust, longing, a young girl on a beach, no, in the sea, no, not a girl, a seal, and not the sea but in a stone room, a cave? The images came so fast and furiously she could hardly breathe, couldn't find her balance.

She had to get out, beyond reach. She dropped down and rolled, she hoped it was the right direction, away and not towards. Suddenly all was quiet, inside and out. Vaguely aware of the uncomfortably rocky ground under her, she lay still, let her heart find its rhythm again. The surface under her was hard and unforgiving. She would probably have a few good bruises by morning. A shadow fell over her, and hands grabbed her upper arms. She opened her eyes. Bren was riled up—she could see his eyes blazing, and she could sense the intensity of his emotions right down to her toes.

"You can get your hands off me and let me get up now," she tried to say with some dignity.

"Like the blazes I will. Christ, what the hell just happened here? What happened to you?!" Bren unconsciously shook her.

"Let me go!" Maddy managed to get out through gritted teeth. He'd seen her, was front and center witness to her succumbing to one of the strongest visions she'd had in a very long time. She was humiliated beyond bearing, and it looked like Bren wasn't too happy either. Fear, embarrassment and the need to have time and space to process it all was first and foremost. What could he be thinking of her? Fear, disgust? She needed to end it right here, before she hurt even more than she did at the moment, both physically and emotionally. When they came that strong, that unexpectedly, they took a physical toll on her body, and now there would be humiliation as well.

Bren looked down at his hands, gripping her arms. He'd seen her go, saw her turn white and just go. Her eyes had gone glassy, then she simply dropped away. No other way to describe it. His instinct was to pull her back, to hold on to her, for himself, for her safety. As soon as he grabbed her his mind went fuzzy, sensed darkness, but it seemed to have passed and was just a vague memory now. Perhaps it was just the haze of fear. He realized she would have bruises from the fall and bruises from his hands, ones he put there on her fair skin trying to hold her, trying to, what? he thought now...rescue her? His hands sprang away. He was mad, at himself more than at her. But what had just happened?

Maddy got up, shakily, found her balance, and started to stride off towards the scrub brush and the path on the other side. She couldn't leave quickly enough. Leaping over stones, barely alighting on solid ground, she practically flew.

Brennan took a few seconds to realize she was fleeing. He called to her. "Maddy, wait... Maddy talk to me... Maddy, for God's sake!" He began to follow behind, stumbling over the damn stones, twisting his ankle and lengthening his stride to try to catch up. "Madeline Murphy, just stop, we've got to talk." Well, he would admit later, that wasn't the most insightful thing to say, but he had to keep a link to her, had to let her know he wasn't just going to let this be.

He arrived at their picnic spot just in time to see the old Rover back up with a jerk, turn around and head down the road.

He put his hands on his knees and took a few deep breaths. He couldn't quite wrap his head around it all. One moment he was on a very promising date with a woman whose company he enjoyed immensely, and the next moment it had all gone pear shaped, worse than pear shaped—it simply imploded. He blamed himself. For Christ's sake, she was hurt and then he'd added to her bruises in his panic. He had to call her, had to talk to her.

He stood and slowly walked to his Rover. How much time to allow for her to get home? He realized he didn't even know exactly where she lived. Well, he would find out, and by the Saints would make her listen. He would apologize, he would grovel, he would do whatever it took. Then he would find out what the hell happened at those stones. There was something more here, something beyond simple research and Maddy was in it knee deep. Well, she would jolly well tell him and then she wasn't going to do whatever it was on her own if he could help it. Bren would make sure of that. The Rover slid into reverse, backed up and carefully turned on to the road, heading back towards Galway. He drove methodically, deliberately, planning, reliving,

circling around and around in his head the events
of the afternoon.

NOW

Maddy pulled onto the drive and parked the old Rover in its usual spot near the garden shed. She put her head on the steering wheel for a few minutes to settle her mind and body. The handle on the car door felt heavy and comfortably solid as she opened it, turned, and set her feet firmly on the ground. Her ground, her home, her safe haven.

She tried to slip in the cottage quietly and serenely—no sense in making a fuss. Hopefully her Gran wouldn't think it odd she was home already. Maddy called to her, but got no answer. Worry started creeping its way into her heart when she spied the older woman asleep in her chair in the parlor. She carefully laid her hand on her shoulder to make sure she was breathing still—yes, nice and steady. Just an afternoon nap, then. Maddy re-tucked the lap blanket gently over her and left as quietly as she had entered.

She hung her satchel in its usual place. Routine was a comfort after such turmoil. *Keep busy, keep busy,* was the mantra going through her head. She ached, she mourned, she tried to put the visions in perspective for what they were telling her, not for how they ruined her day. After putting the kettle on, she rubbed her forehead while getting out willow bark and ginger for tea. Most visions were during sleep, or came through like a soft breeze. This one was a tempest that blew in out of the blue, knocked her for a loop and had her head pounding. The tea would help, and so would a distraction. Baking would do.

She got out flour, yeast, currants, thyme, tested the water on her wrist for just the right temperature and proceeded to make herb bread. There was no better therapy in her mind than pommeling and pounding on yeast dough. One lump of dough was Brennan and his thick manly head. Couldn't he see she had needed understanding and calm, not questions and anger?

She had hoped he would be someone who could see her, see her for who she was. Hoped he'd be someone she could share her true self with. Now she wasn't so sure. On the other hand, a small voice in her head pointed out she wasn't the only one taken by surprise at the reaction. He'd been as shaken as she had been, maybe more so, said that little voice.

She had set her mobile on the little doily-covered table by the door, next to the African violets her Gran was so fond of. It chimed several times, then chirped to signify a voicemail. She tried to ignore it. Her hands were covered in dough and flour, otherwise she would simply turn it off. She knew it would be Brennan. Well, she had nothing to say to him right now, and maybe not ever. That little voice of reason in her head could just stop niggling at her as well. A handful of dough slammed onto the bread board.

Just as she was forming the loaves to rise and laying a linen cloth over, the phone chirped again. *Well, for all the saints and glory's sake, could ye not just let it be,* she thought. This time he left a text message; she could tell by the sound. The loaves were tucked up with extra care, an apology of sorts as they had taken such a load of her anger. She washed her hands, the bright scent of the seaside soap reminding her to breathe deeply and allow her headache to loosen its grip. She had been ridiculed before, subjected to anger and disbelief before, rejected by her own mum, and had survived. Thanks to her Gran, she not only survived, but learned to thrive and treasure her gift. She had begun to care very much, too much perhaps, for the handsome professor with the dark eyes and quick wit. Even if he hadn't been prepared for what had happened, even if he could be made to understand, she'd make sure he wouldn't put this ache in her heart again. Too risky.

Brennan pushed *end call* and slumped back in his favorite reading chair. Women, who could figure them out? This one had him all tied up in knots, and it was not a pleasant feeling. In fact, it really sucked. He tossed his mobile onto the side table and got up. He paced and stewed. He'd called, he'd emailed, he'd texted—what more could he do? He grabbed his trainers, threw on a ratty pair of shorts and his favorite "Kiss me I'm Irish" Tee shirt, clipped his keys to his inner belt loop, and headed out the door for a run.

Sweaty, determined and guilt-ridden, he opened the door to his apartment just in time to hear his phone ring. Finally, she had come to her senses! As he grabbed the phone from the side table, he saw it was his sister Erin. He answered, but disappointment had him stymied for a moment.

"Bren, are you there?" He heard Erin say.

"Yeah, give me a few, I've just come in from a run." He whipped his sweat-soaked shirt off over his head, wiped his face with it, tossed it towards his bedroom and walked towards the fridge with the phone to his ear.

"Okay, I'm here," he said as he grabbed a bottle of Harp and popped the top.

"Well?" Erin drew out the word as if it had multiple syllables.

"Well, what?" He decided to play dumb to stall for time. He'd tell her, but make her work for it, he thought. His frustration at all womenkind at the moment was a broad brush. He settled back into his reading chair, stretched his legs out.

"How did your date with the charming Madeline go?" Erin wondered why he was being so obtuse, and it showed in her voice.

"If you must know, it started out grand. It ended as a disaster." Bren ran his hand through his hair, turned and draped a leg over the arm of the chair. He took a long swig of the Harp.

Erin was quietly waiting on the other end for more.

"The picnic was perfect, then we went to see some ancient standing stone ruins. They were just a short hike away. One minute Maddy was just in front of me, heading over the stoney field. She got there ahead of me by a mere minute, canna have been much more. I watched her put her hand on one of the uprights." He ran a hand over his face, remembering the confusion, the terror. "And then, I swear Erin, she just went white, her eyes rolled back, she staggered, wrapped her arms around herself and dropped to the ground. I thought she was having some food poisoning attack, or some seizure, or... I don't know what. I bent down and grabbed her, shook her. Christ, Erin, in my panic, I must have put bruises on her arms." He stood to pace, to think it through as he talked. "Something happened, I still don't know what, something that shook her to her soul, shook me too. She asked me to let go and when I did, she fled. Her car was pulling out of the field when I got there. I just missed her. I've called, I've emailed, I've texted, and nothing. I have to talk to her, have to get her to understand. I feel sick about it, how I reacted. Jezus Erin, I think I even yelled at her." He stopped. What more could he say?

"I see," said Erin, "and you're not sick from the food? So it's not that. And after she went down and you reacted so, shall we say, 'strongly,' she didn't want to hang around to have a nice cozy chat about it? I can well understand that part. You got scared, which came through as anger, so she's probably embarrassed. And now ye want to make it right, bring her flowers, sweet talk and grovel. Well, I've a few things to say, if you care to listen."

"I'm not surprised—let me have it then. I'm not in the best mood, but I'll listen to whatever you want to dish out." Erin was an excellent journalist and he'd come to realize that her insights in her writing, and now in her personal perspectives were mostly right on.

"Were you in the doghouse much with Christine?" This was a surprising direction for Erin to take. He wondered where she was going but decided to go along. He didn't have much choice, or other options, and he was a desperate man.

"All the time at the end. I practically had my mail delivered there."

"Aside from the guilt about the bruises, and I know you'd not knowingly hurt any woman, did you feel this same kind of desperate panic to do whatever it would take to sort it all out and make things right with Christine?"

Erin had a point. In the beginning, when he and Christine were at odds he'd offer up a bauble, a bouquet or dinner out—pretty tepid in hindsight—but he understood now that their emotional connection wasn't all that deep, so it was that easy to smooth over the rough bits. There was never this intense need to be forgiven, be understood, to do whatever he could to be back in her good graces.

Bren's silence spoke volumes. "I thought so," said Erin. She decided to just let that one soak into his thick head. "One other thing occurs to me." She paused, as if wondering how to phrase it. "Bren, you said she's a fascination to you and I'd bet it's not just her looks. With Christine it was all: *she's beautiful and smart blah blah blah*. All surface stuff of infatuation and testosterone."

"Jezus, Erin," Bren cut in. "We were young and thought we were in love. We, or at least I, thought that was love."

"Yeah, yeah." Erin dismissed his excuses.

"But, listen, when you talk about Maddy it seems different. Yeah, okay, you're older and maybe wiser, though the jury could still be out on that... but I am going to go out on a limb here, so bear with me. You love Irish history, its myth and magic, its drama and resilience. She's asked for your help with a subject you live and breathe. So already there's a connection there that perhaps runs deeper than infatuation and testosterone. Beyond that you've got a feel, a sense that she's something more. So, she touched the auld stone and went all crackers. You, of all people, with your Irish history background, your fascination with the scope of it should know. Put that brilliant mind of yours to work here, think out of the box. What if she has a gift, a sense of things most don't. Now, I bet she thinks you're either angry or afraid of her or both." She let that hang for a moment. "Were you afraid of her, or afraid for her?"

"Afraid? Not for me, no, nothing to be afraid of for me. I was focused all on her, was she ill, was she all right, was she having some kind of panic attack.

I felt so helpless." He reflected a moment. Erin was silent, letting him come to his own conclusions.

Pacing again, he started muttering to himself. "You think she felt something, saw something? Like a vision?" He closed his eyes, ran his hand through his hair, replaying the afternoon, kept muttering. "Some echo from the past, the stones are more than ancient, plenty of history stored up there. Maybe the legend about the crazy Abbot is more truth than lore. Darkness and harm could have, would have, stained those stones."

Erin continued to listen patiently.

Then, as if remembering she was on the other end of the line, "Christ, Erin, I'm an eejit."

"Yep" was her concise reply.

"I've got to talk to her, let her know." *Let her know what?* he thought. That if that is what happened, he would accept and treasure her unique ability to see beyond, that it was as much a part of her as her laugh, her smile, her wit and her thoughtfulness. Was this, then, as Erin had said, not just infatuation and lust but a gut level, inexplicable, sense of connection? He turned the idea around in his head. Yes, he had to admit, his feelings for Maddy went deep. It had been fast, and stealthy. He wasn't even looking for it. He was a busy professor, with a good life, plenty of social time when he wanted, and plenty of solitary time when he wanted. In his experience, you put a woman into the mix for the long-term, and your life gets complicated in a hurry. But this one came out of nowhere and hit him right in the solar plexus. He'd gladly take all the complications if she would only let him.

"Bren." Erin's voice on the other end of the mobile line brought him back. "Have you figured it out then? That she means more than lust and looks?"

"Yeah, I think I just got that part, thanks." He said it a bit sarcastically. He knew Erin wouldn't take it personally, and in fact was probably congratulating herself for leading him to that conclusion like a trained pony.

"So, what are you going to do about it?"

"I've already told you, I've tried to reach her, and she won't have any part of it."

"And you're going to give up, just like that? I have more faith in you than that. You should have more faith in yourself. Maybe you should think about showing up on her doorstep and not leaving until she listens?"

"Feck all, Erin, I have no idea where she lives exactly. Somewhere near the coast. I know she commuted to her classes at Uni, so not so far, yeah, but that leaves a lot of ground to cover."

"And there's no one else who would know, no one else to get to help ye?"

"She got in touch with me through a former Professor, Ian Finegal, but he's in New Zealand at the moment. I could email him... but she lives with her Gran, and I did talk to her once when I called." Bren caught himself. He'd not reached her mobile then and had tried another number that he was sure must have been their home phone. He prayed he hadn't inadvertently gotten rid of his call history; the number might still be in there. Or maybe it was on the business card she had given him. He walked over to his desk, with the phone still to his ear, and started flipping through piles of notes, shifting papers and books. He knew he'd tucked it somewhere.

"Erin, I've got to go. I think I know where I might have her Gran's number." He glanced casually at his desk clock. "It's too late to call tonight, and I'll let Maddy have some recovery time, but first thing in the morning for sure."

"You'll let me know, yeah."

Sisters, Bren thought, *nosey as hell*. "You're such a nosey Parker." He spoke his thought out loud. But she meant well.

"And when you get it all sorted, I want to meet this paragon who might put up with the likes of you, okay?"

"Of course," said Bren absently, hoping Maddy would indeed 'put up with the likes of him'. He was anxious now to get Erin off the phone and find that number.

After a bit more rummaging around he remembered he had tucked it under the crystal pen holder on his desk. He held it tightly between two fingers, saw two phone numbers below her email. *Aha*, he thought. *I've got you now.*

He whistled while he heated up left over curry and rice, confident in his powers of persuasion. If he could get her Gran in his corner, Maddy didn't stand a chance.

Maddy had a brief and evasive conversation with her Gran about the date with Bren. She suspected that Gran knew something was awry but thankfully hadn't pried. They had enjoyed the bread with cheese and a nice salad of summer greens and herbs. Gran was feeling a wee bit better, but still tired easily and went to bed early. Maddy had stayed up, puttering around, making lists of things that needed doing over the next week, checking supplies for making scones, lemon and thyme shortbread and other baked goods the local stores were always asking for. Tourist season was heading into full swing, and she did not want to disappoint her friends who depended on her goods for business.

While she puttered and organized her supplies, her mind wandered. Deciphering the visions had to take precedence over her emotional turmoil. Maybe that was a cop-out, avoiding her own turmoil. As the old adage went: 'you should pick your battles,' and so the tug of war between her heart and her head where Brennan was concerned would just have to wait. The mystery in the jar of dirt had been waiting ever so much longer.

Texts and emails from 'himself' were like a leaky faucet, something you knew you needed to deal with, but weren't ready to face. She was determined to ignore them. Otherwise, she appreciated technology and the internet for access to all kinds of information. She had gone online and typed in mystical ruins near Galway—a long shot, but worth a try. History of the ruined monastery and mysterious tower of Kilneamh came up, with a very obscure link to a legend of an Abbot who was excommunicated from Rome under very suspicious circumstances. Hmmm... Might be worth a bit more digging on that one. The old clock in the hallway chimed eleven. Suddenly the events of the day and the toll on her body, physically and emotionally, caught up with her. Time to shut the research down and rest her mind and body.

Maddy slept fitfully. Dreams of caves, and towers, and mad monks intermingled with dreams of Brennan calling to her, echoing in the caverns. Someone needed her help. By morning, she was the one who needed help. A hot shower, her favorite jeans and tee, and two cups of strong coffee, and she was feeling a bit more focused and ready to take on the day. Her list from the night before was on the kitchen table.

Gran had come down, fully dressed, fully rested, cheery as ever. Maddy tried to put on an equally upbeat face.

"I'm headed to town for a few things— is there anything you'd like me to pick up for you while I'm out?" she asked her Gran as she set a cup of tea out for her.

"No, child, I'm fine, but if ye could drop off some flowers to the church on your way, I'd appreciate it. I've some nice Veronica, star flower and lavender. I'll cut it now and have it ready for ye when ye go." She took a final sip of her tea, took the cup to the sink and with her garden basket and scissors in hand, stepped out to the side garden.

Maddy had only been gone a few minutes when the phone rang. Gran finished filling the Waterford vase her Frank had given her with some of the fresh-picked flowers, dried her hands, and went to answer.

"Hello," she said tentatively. Maddy was always fussing about those market fellas that wanted ye to buy something, or take some survey, or worse, take yer money. She knew it was all a hum, but felt bad for them. Who would want people hanging up on them all day? She tried to humor them, and be polite and gracious.

"Ah, is this Madeline's Gran, then?" It was Maddy's professor fella; she recognized the voice.

She knew something had happened, but hadn't pressed her granddaughter about it. It was still a tender spot, and experience told the older woman to wait a bit to prod and pry. Her young fella was a different matter altogether.

"Yes, and would this be Professor O'Connor himself? And please call me Annie —it's Annie Donahue to be proper I suppose."

Now that he had Maddy's relative on the phone, his confidence wavered just a bit. She was blood kin after all. Would she champion his cause? How much to explain?

"Um, Mrs. Donahue... Annie, would you be knowing that Madeline and I met for lunch yesterday?"

"Yes, I did know and as she is currently out on an errand, I don't mind telling ye that I also know it did not end well. Naught has been said, she's been tight as a clam at low tide. If it is on your shoulders, young man, you have a lot to answer for! Madeline's been through enough already in her life, she didna need more heartache. I had such hopes for ye, too." She drifted off and Bren saw his chance to get a word in before he felt even lower.

"I will take some of the blame, but not all, no. There was a... misunderstanding, I guess you would say. I've been trying to get in touch with Maddy to talk to her about it, and she's not answering. I was hoping I could ask you for some help there." Bren crossed his fingers and his toes and sent a prayer upward. He wasn't overly religious, but you couldn't grow up in Ireland without having some ingrained spiritual inclination.

In his nervousness he babbled on. "I find I am..." (*not ready to go there*, he thought) "...well, I find that I care quite a bit for your granddaughter, and she gave me quite a start yesterday when we went to see some standing stones near Galway. I didn't react well, and I'm afraid she has probably come to conclusions that don't show me in the best of light. I meant well, and frankly, she had me scared beyond thinking clearly. I need to apologize and ask her to see it from my perspective. If she is still not wishing to talk to me after, I'll honor that, but I'm hoping she'll forgive me."

Gran thought for a minute. Brennan waited with bated breath on the other end of the line. He seemed sincere. "Yes, I will help ye, but if you so much as hurt that child's heart, you will have the likes of me to answer to young man. Now, why don't you plan to come for dinner, if ye can, 6 o'clock sharp. Madeline will no be tossin' ye out if I've invited ye. Ye can have a chance to say your piece, and we'll see what's what after that."

Gran gave Brennan directions, although he insisted all he needed was their address and he would put it into that new-fangled thingy that told you where to go. Annie thought to herself it would be handy to have one as she'd like to tell some folks where to go, but didn't think that new-fangled device could tell them how to get *there*. Still, she admitted to herself, most folks who were destined in that direction would probably find it themselves anyway.

Madeline had taken advantage of her time in town and the drive there and back to talk herself into a more even keel. She couldn't think about Brennan with a clear head, so she set him aside in her mind for later. It was most important now to concentrate on what she had learned about the Abbot, the monastery, and how that may relate to the mystery in the jar. She had her work cut out for her there, and with tourist season coming into full speed, she would be more than busy enough. No sense trying to add an overbearing man into the mix. She could see now that he was assuredly unprepared for her extreme reaction to connecting with the stone. And, if she was honest, she'd not been prepared for such a strong response. It was the violence and intensity of this one that was most unexpected and that had quite shaken her up. This intensified her reaction to him, to the situation, to her embarrassment. And, too, seen from his point of view, he was probably scared. Whether for her or of her was hard to be certain about, although her gut instinct leaned towards the more benevolent version. She'd think about being in touch with him, to explain and apologize. Just not yet.

Several baskets of staple goods were set on the table, her keys and mobile set by the violets near the door. Maddy twisted her hair into a quick bun on top of her head and clipped it. When she'd stopped by her friend Erin's tea shop, she'd gotten an order for an extra 3 dozen scones, and then Maureen from the gift shop next door saw her and ran over to ask for more soap. It was good to see these women, who had become her friends, doing so well. Friendship had been a scarce commodity when Maddy was growing up. In more recent years, as she grew more confident about herself, she found it easier to find her place, make treasured connections with other women her age. There was comfort in that.

She was humming an old Irish lilt and putting the groceries away when her Gran came into the kitchen.

"And how is my favorite Gran?" asked Maddy, striving to maintain a cheerful manner.

"Aye, I'll do. And how's my best granddaughter?" countered the older woman.

"I've more orders from Erin and from Maureen. The tourists are coming in by the busloads and spending money like it was water through their fingers. Imagine that. They need..." Maddy had grabbed the French linen apron from behind the pantry door and paused as she tied it around her waist when her Gran stopped her in mid-stream.

"Yer man called and I've invited him to come for dinner. Do ye think we can thaw out some of that nice salmon young Alfred gave us?" Alfred was the son of a neighbor and fished off the coast of Galway. He often brought them some of his bounty when he came home for a visit.

Maddy sat down hard on the straight-backed chair at the kitchen table and shook her head ever so slightly. "He called?" Clearly he did, so that was a stupid question. "Gran," she sighed, "He..." How to explain? And how much to explain? "We aren't...

I'm not ready to..." She began. She was abruptly cut off.

"Madeline Mackenzie Murphy, you listen to me now." Gran grabbed an earlobe and tugged gently. "God dinna give you these two things on the side of yer head just for hanging decoration. You'll use them to listen to him and give him a chance to explain. 'Tis only fair, and ye know it. He's fair torn up about what happened. I've no asked, but I can see plain as day that something went amiss there, and you've a chance to make it right again." Although they hadn't spoken of it directly, she knew about Maddy's research, her desire to discover and solve a deeper mystery buried in Belinda's jar of dirt. But this time, as far as she was concerned, answers in the past could wait. "How can ye right an auld wrong if ye won't take care of the one starin' ye in the face?"

Maddy took a deep breath. Her Gran was right. It was only fair, and she'd known it. Wasn't she just thinking she'd be in touch, make amends? Let him have his say. She just hadn't thought it would be so soon. She really wasn't quite finished feeling sorry for herself.

Well, *done is done*, as her Gran often said, so no use adding to the fuss.

"I'll go get the salmon and set it to thaw. We've greens and some herb bread left. I can do a quick tart as well. If I need to listen it may as well be on a full stomach."

THEN

Patience is generally considered a virtue. For the Abbot, patience was just a necessary means to an end. He'd learned the old woman called the child Ula. How fitting, as it meant 'a jewel of the sea'. He liked jewels and this was a rare one indeed. One he was most desirous of adding to his collection.

The church demanded tithes each year, paid to assure entrance to heaven. A tithe was supposed to be one-tenth of a worker's income or worth, and if you didn't have silver or gold coin, grains, woven cloth, parchment, produce, livestock or fish were accepted instead. The Abbot would often find fault wherever he could with the lowlier offerings. The grain looked moldy, the fish were old, the livestock sickly, and on and on, reducing the value of the goods. Only the best would pass his muster, and even those were sometimes looked down upon. Once he gave the nod of approval, the monk appointed to be clerk would mark the register with who gave and what the value was deemed to be. The Abbot cared little about what happened to the farm produce or livestock offerings afterward. Some went to the kitchens for the monastery, the prime bits culled out for his own discerning palate. The grains were stored in the old round tower, an ancient leftover monstrosity from the days of Viking raids. The only entrance was 8 meters up, and lifting the sacks of grains, kegs of ale, wine or any other items for storage was a major production.

If a pilgrim or local merchant happened to offer up something of more value, a coin, a gold ring or jewel, they would receive immediate blessings and a personal benediction and assured a front row seat in the kingdom of heavenly delights. These prized offerings were set aside in a small leather chest, conveniently positioned right next to the Abbot.

Moira brought her weaving and tanned hides to cover her tithe. Even when Hugh was alive this annual ritual made her nervous. She had heard rumors that the Abbot himself had a particular interest in Ula, and this made Moira even more on edge this year. She was not against tithing in principle. In her world, the church held the keys to the entrance to heaven. Surely, she thought, there must be other doors, doors that were more concerned with kindness, benevolence and goodness rather than goods from hard labors. These were not thoughts to be uttered, however, and she strove to keep her head down, be pious and obedient and not risk any undue notice.

When her turn came in line, she handed over her cart full of hides and cloth. The Abbot looked straight at her with a speculative eye as he fingered the fine woolens half-heartedly and nodded. Under her eyes she saw that the Abbot's eyes weren't focused on the task at hand, but rather into the distance, towards the sea. The scribe never looked up as he noted numbers in his ledger.

That look, the speculation, the calculation in it, had given Moira shivers. Then, the look was gone, the Abbot already showing vague interest in the cart behind her. With an imperious wave of dismissal from the scribe she turned her own cart around and headed straight home. As the cart clattered on the rough ground behind her, she reflected on those she dealt with—the butcher, the blacksmith and neighbors. They all liked Ula, asked about her in a kind way, occasionally even gave Moira extra treats for the young girl and didn't question her appearance. To them it was clearly a blessing from God that provided the widow with some help and company. The Abbot's interest, however, was for reasons that she feared were not Holy ones, nor stemming from concern for her personal comfort and welfare.

It had taken months of patience and coaxing to get Ula up the path and away from the beach to Moria's small holding. Esthwyn was right: trust added to curiosity finally won out. Once Ula saw the animals, fed the goats, petted the sheep and even made friends with the cat, she was eager to visit again. In the beginning, Moria would meet her on the beach, and they would walk while Moira would teach the young girl words. Now, they conversed more and used their hands less to communicate. It didn't take long, however, for Ula to be running ahead of Moira up the path to the little farmstead, her limber legs almost dancing, her feet barely touching the ground and her long silky hair flowing and glinting in the sun like quicksilver.

When Moira had come down with a fever and barely had the strength to feed the animals and none for her walk to the beach, Ula came looking for her. Once she saw that the older woman was ailing, and unable to manage fully for herself, she stayed to help. Moira had no idea what exactly had happened to Ula's sea-born family... they each just accepted and didn't question what the fates had offered. Moira had the daughter she never thought to have, and Ula had a mother with two legs and a life in another realm of this earth. Occasionally Ula would disappear for a day or two. At first Moira worried. Ula learned to let her earth mother know when she felt the need for water-when the sea called her spirit.

In this loving and accepting environment, Ula grew and flourished. She became friends with Esthwyn and her family, as Moira had hoped. When Alfred, the oldest son, would come back with his father from a fishing trip, he would always bring a salmon to Moira and Ula. The first time he did this he saw Ula's eyes light up. She loved fish. After that, Alfred habitually brought something from the sea for her. It was usually from their catch, but once in a while it would be a shell, or marbled agate smoothed by the relentless stroke of the waves.

Ula had been inside the hut, preparing the most recent offering from Alfred, and waiting for Moira to come back from town when the Abbot's guards came by. The three men were in black with chainmail tunics and armed with crossbows. They boldly rode their steeds up to the gate, then silently scanned the small yard. These fearsome men were not unknown to her as she'd seen them around the market, or galloping down the road, clouds of dust in their wake. Never, though, had she been so close. Never before had they stopped so pointedly at their croft. Moira had taught her to be humble and reserved in the presence of any who served the Abbot, and therefore God himself.

Ula stepped up to the door and did a slight curtsey with a bowed head. She stood, waiting to see what these minions of the Abbot would do and wondering what she would or should do in response, if pressed.

Fortunately, the one clearly in charge just nodded in return, which seemed to signal the others as they, in unison, wheeled their horses around and thundered back down the road.

NOW

Brennan had never before worried about a date, but this was not an ordinary dinner date-this was a 'get back on firmer ground' date. Should he bring a gift? If so, what? Were flowers sufficient? He dismissed that idea as Maddy had talked of her Gran's flower gardens and her own herb beds. Wouldn't that be like bringing coals to Newcastle? He didn't have much time, and yet it felt like the day loomed in front of him. He called his sister Erin.

"Bren. What's up?" answered Erin succinctly.

"I spoke with her Gran." (No need to explain whose Gran). "Maddy was out, but she, not Maddy—her Gran—invited me to dinner."

"That's brilliant then, yeah?" replied his sister.

"Yeah, 'tis, but it's tonight—what do I bring? Flowers don't seem right; they have their own gardens, although I think I'll bring some for her Gran anyway, to be polite, but for Maddy? Sweets are too, well, cliched and common, jewelry seems a bit presumptive at the moment... and, God's sake, I can't think." Bren floundered, definitely in trouble here.

"Ah, like that is it... thinkin' jewelry are you?" There was a poignant pause on the other end. "Oh, wait, I'm having a vision. It's... Oh God." Her voice dropped to a dramatic whisper. "It's a ring in a box." She heard him make a cross between a growl and a choking sound on the other end of the line. "Ah well, that may be puttin' the old cart in front of the horse." She laughed at the dig, then let it hang.

"Erin..." Bren practically growled again. "That horse isn't anywhere near the barn, or the cart. We've not even had a proper first date."

"Just kidding. So, let's see, you need something unique, something that shows you had her in mind, have her rethinking her opinion. How about some artifact, or something to show her that you're an Irish history nut. How about..."

Bren cut her off. "Brilliant! I got it, thanks! Gotta go, love ya, brat." He hung up. Erin looked at her mobile and thought about calling back and getting on him for being rude, but she supposed he had good cause, and besides, she would grill him thoroughly tomorrow morning. She put it on her mobile calendar: "Bren-deets."

Bren went straight away to the library corner of his flat. Floor to ceiling books on shelves, stacked in front of the others with larger books overflowing on the side tables. He moved one strategically placed stack out of the way to expose a glass enclosure where the special volumes were hidden including a small collection of Medieval manuscripts, antiquarian books on Irish History and rare ephemera on Celtic culture. He carefully fingered through the leather hand-bound spines until he found the one he knew was perfect. *Sir James Ware's Herbal*, written in 1786. It was in decent condition for its age, and he knew instinctively that Maddy would treat it with the respect and care it needed. He figured if his plan worked, he wasn't losing a book, he was gaining a future.

He was not one to stockpile wrappings and trimmings, as he'd learned long ago to depend on the shops where presents were purchased to do the honors. So, what to wrap the book in? He scanned his flat for inspiration. A cloth bag from the Bodleian library hung on a hook on the back of his kitchen door. He'd bought it on a trip to Oxford when he was doing research. It turned out to be a useful size to transport a couple of brews when he was doing errands on his bike. He took it down and checked the inside for presentability. No spills or sticky residue. Sniffed it just to make sure. Good, no skanky beer smell. He wrapped the book in a clean linen dish cloth and tucked it in the bag. It would have to do.

It was a bit after six when he pulled down the lane to the stone cottage with white shutters. A small porch extended from the red door. Front porches were unusual in Ireland, especially for a cottage like this, but somehow it fit and made it seem all the more welcoming. He hoped he would indeed be welcome. He was assured that good manners, at least, would mean Maddy wouldn't send him home without dinner or that he wouldn't have a chance to have his say. And there was the crux of it: what would he say? What *should* he say? He'd thought all day about how to explain, how to make amends.

Maddy was genuine, simple, not simple minded by any means, but he knew instinctively she didn't want or need a lot of fancy trimmings, glitter or gloss, just the truth, spoken from the heart. Christine would have demanded, indeed expected, the glitter and gloss to smooth the way. Not Maddy. He was confident the Herbal was the right choice. An offering, sure, a gift of apology, absolutely, but he also saw it as insurance, putting a bit of grease on the hinges to open her heart, so to speak.

Maddy had topped the salmon with lemon, butter, rosemary and dill. It was now resting in its clay baking dish, in the fridge, next to the salad and raspberry tart. She glanced up at the wall clock. Nearing to five—ah, plenty of time to do a bit of tidy up, calm her mind and soul, and prepare for their guest. She'd shooed Gran out of the kitchen, out from underfoot, to the garden to cut flowers for the table. The windows were open, the cotton curtains with hand tatted lace edging billowing slightly with the breeze. Maddy could hear the older woman humming, talking to the plants, or perhaps to herself. No doubt she was pleased with her part in orchestrating this particular social event. Truth be told, Maddy was now grateful for that meddling.

She could admit now, see now, that she was as culpable as Brennan for the fallout from their picnic. Firstly, her reaction was based on old patterns, expecting him to reject her as a freak like her mother had. Then, there was holding her purpose and mission to herself and not fully disclosing her part in the mystery resting in the jar on the mantel. She'd asked for his help without fully letting him in on the secret, on her secret, and it weighed heavily on her mind. Perhaps it was time to open up to Bren and take the chance he would understand, more than understand... accept. As she straightened pillows, tucked knitting in the basket at the foot of the rocking chair, put books back on the shelf to the left of the fireplace, she glanced at the jar and reached for it. Held it gingerly. To others, simply a jar of dirt, unremarkable, and utterly silent. Who else would see or feel beyond the obvious to the essence of its history, to the pulse of the past deep within. Just dirt, wash it off your hands, shake it out of the woven rugs, dump it in a clay pot with seeds and water to nurture the new. But what about the old? What about what is remembered, indeed, embedded, in those grains of sand and soil? She sighed. "Working on it," she assured herself and whatever lay silently in the jar, then put it carefully back on the mantel next to the impish leprechaun from Tipperary.

In her bedroom under the eaves, she changed into black linen pants, and an ecru tee, fancied up with delicate embroidery along the neck edge, then did a quick braid of her hair, twisted it up, anchored it with a sliver clip, and went back down the stairs.

Bren was just about to knock at the door as Gran came around the corner on a well-worn path from the back garden. She had an arm full of flowers. He went quickly back down the steps to help her. His own offering of flowers in one hand, the book bag over his arm.

"Can I give you a hand there Mrs. Donahue?" He held his free hand out to her.

"Ah, ye must be Maddy's Professor then. Right on time, I like that in a young man." As she'd not a watch on that Bren could see, he wasn't sure how she knew he was punctual, but figured he wouldn't argue. As his football coach used to say: "If it's a point in your favor, don't argue with the referee."

"I've got the flowers just fine but if ye could give me a hand up the steps, now. My knees aren't as reliable at the end of the day." She lifted her free arm up and out for him to give support as she took the steps one by one.

"I can see I'd not have bothered with flowers. Yours are grander than these."

"Now, don't be daft—a woman always likes a gift, and your flowers are just fine, thank you very much," said Gran with a nod and glint of approval in her eyes. Yes, she and Maddy's young man were going to get along just fine.

Maddy watched from the parlor as Bren carefully matched his steps with the older woman's as they worked their way to the door. She had a feeling about this man, not looked for, not asked for, but there nonetheless, and one she needed to accept and trust. His innate kindness, his heart and his canny brain. To teach, to listen, to see beyond, beneath the surface to the roots of Irish history and culture. All attributes in his favor. Fit and good looking? Well, that was a bonus, wasn't it now?

Smiling at that thought, she opened the door and greeted them both. "Welcome to our cottage, Bren. Now hand over the flowers and I'll go put them in some water. After I get them taken care of, I'll put the salmon in the oven. Why don't the two of you make yourselves comfortable in the parlor."

Bren took a chance and leaned over to kiss her cheek while her hands were full of the flowers and holding the door open.

"Thank you both for letting me come to dinner. I've not had a home cooked meal for ages. It's a welcome change from take away or the pub."

Gran spoke right up. "'Tis grand of ye to come on such short notice. Now, off with ye Maddy, I'm going to enjoy the company of this young fella of yours while ye get sorted out in the kitchen." And just like that she was dismissed.

The two ambled off into the parlor. Maddy smiled again. One more point in his favor, he was kind and considerate of her Gran. Her hand on Brennan's arm, he led her into the parlor just like a fine lady being taken into a fancy dinner. He could be in a tuxedo rather than the more casual oxford shirt, tweed vest and Khakis. An innate air of good breeding was in the man, not the clothes. He didn't seem out of place, as she knew right away that he would be as comfortable in a formal stately home as he was right here in their cottage. What was she doing? A simple girl, from a ramshackle background with an odd trait and here was this handsome devil clearly from another class altogether. Some would boast that the class system was gone in Ireland, but deep down you didn't erase generations of breeding, manners and polish. It was in your very DNA.

Once she'd gotten past her own baggage, she'd forgiven his reaction, could understand it better. And besides, the fates had thrown them together, for better or for worse, she would follow her heart wherever it led, fool's errand not to. She listened to the two settle into the parlor and chat softly, then sighed. Best to set her musings aside and get in the kitchen.

Conversation over dinner was convivial and enlightening. Gran did her best to wheedle as much information out of their guest as she could, and not always as subtly as Maddy would have liked. Several pointed questions had her cringing. Bren would look over and wink, take a leisurely sip of his wine, and answer as best he could with grace and aplomb.

Had he been married before?;
Yes, but briefly. A college connection when he and she were young and clueless. She'd moved on before he did, but he was still just as culpable in his mind. They had not been as comfortable with each other as time passed, realizing they had very different views of their future. His fault as much as hers for not discussing it enough, or at all, really. He hoped she was as happy and content with her life now as he was with his.

Ye've siblings then?

Yes, a younger sister, Erin.

They live in Galway?

No, south of Dublin in County Wicklow. His father was a country attorney who liked to raise sheep. His mother, very involved with the local schools and library. Catholic, of course, but not strict about it. He had gone to public school, then Trinity, then graduate work at Oxford. An impressive education by anyone's standards.

He and Gran nattered on about Irish history, how it goes deep and is part of who you are as a person and as a culture. Maddy listened, enjoyed the repartee, passed the food, cleared the table, brought out the tart and the coffee, and a small carafe of Port, just in case Bren preferred it. She found she didn't have to contribute much —a nod here and there, an occasional opinion when asked. Finally, chairs were pushed back, as Gran announced she was about done in for the day and would leave the two of them to tidy up. She took Brennan's hand, patted it and told him he was a fine young man, and he was welcome anytime.

"I have a feeling you don't suffer fools easily, Mrs. Donahue—Annie," he corrected when she gave him a look, "so I'll consider that quite a compliment."

She gave him a nod. "It is and ye may as well be callin' me Gran. I've a feeling you'll be here more often than not." She smiled like a cat who'd licked the cream pot.

"I know you will be doing right by my granddaughter. She's a special woman, who deserves someone who will appreciate all her talents." Thankfully Gran left it at that and turned to head up the stairs.

Maddy rolled her eyes, turned and gave her a kiss on the cheek. "Good night Gran, sleep well."

Gran smiled at her and tugged at Maddy's ear, whispering, "Put these to good use now."

"I will," she assured her, and watched as Gran slipped slowly, gracefully, up the stairs.

The two worked well together in the kitchen. Clearing, putting away the leftover food, chatting about little things. Bren complimented her culinary skills, and how easy she made everything seem. He admitted he could maybe make a decent Shepherd's Pie, but the kitchen looked a sight after. How so many pots could end up being dirtied for a one dish meal could surely qualify for a physics grant, or ergonomics study. Maddy laughed and just tossed a dish towel his way, offering to give him a lesson or two on kitchen management.

Suddenly they both looked around the kitchen. Bren had flung the dish towel over his right shoulder and was sliding it down to wipe his hands. Maddy found herself watching those capable hands with more in mind than was probably prudent at the moment. All the dishes were done and put away, the little food that was left over was in takeaway containers for Bren. Maddy did not take no for an answer, and he didn't put up too much of an argument on that front.

"How about we sit on the front porch for a bit?" suggested Bren. "The air will feel good, but it's turned cool, and I think there is just a bit of a fog, so maybe if you've a shawl or jumper?"

Time had come for the purpose behind all her Gran's scheming.

"I've a shawl, and I've got something else to show you that's in the parlor, so I'll get those, shall I, and meet you out front?"

Bren nodded, said he also had something he left in the front parlor, following her past the dining room, he to get the book in the linen cloth, she to get the jar.

He waited and held the door for her, book bag tucked under his arm when she returned with a jar in her hand, a softly woven shawl, lifted from the back of the rocking chair, thrown over her shoulders.

They settled on the top step. Maddy looked out to the yard and beyond. The hedge past the front flower bed was barely visible in the softening light and fog.

Bren set the book bag down on the lower step and put his arms on his knees, looking out as well. His rolled back cuffs gave him the appearance of ease, but Maddy could sense his tension, even without touching him. He tipped his head down and took a breath.

"I've been thinking how to apologize." He paused to rub his face, run his hands through his hair. "Straight up is usually the best I suppose." He looked up, straight at her and took the hand that had been resting around the jar on her lap just where the edges of her shawl met. "So, Madeline Murphy, please forgive me for behaving like a big lump-headed brute. I, well, I was scared, that's all I can say. I don't know what happened exactly, but I know I hurt you in more ways than one. I know, and I will forever be ashamed for what I did, for how I reacted. Can you give me another chance?"

Maddy looked at him straight on as well, and turned her hand so it held his instead. "I've been thinking, too, about how to apologize, and yes, you're right—straight up it is. You've no need to be ashamed; I am as much to blame. Brennan O'Connor, can you find it in your heart to forgive *me* for not being honest from the start? For not trusting you with the whole story, with the whole of who and what I am and the task I have taken on?"

He raised her hand and kissed the back. "Maddy, you've no need to ask for forgiveness, but if it will make you happy, and God knows I am all for that, then, yes—let's start anew, shall we?"

"Not anew." Brennan's face fell slightly at that. "Lessons learned and hard won make you stronger." She bumped her shoulder against his. "I am sure your football coach would have told you that. God knows, when I first came to live with my Gran, she sang that tune until I was near sick of it—but she had the right of it, you know. Learn from your mistakes and from the injustices of others, so you don't repeat them yourself, but take them to heart."

She slipped her hand out from his and lifted the jar.

"It all starts with this, or at least this particular journey does." She held it out to him.

Bren found himself holding an old Tesco Marmalade jar full of dirt.

"Okay, I may be missing something here, but it looks like a jar of dirt, yeah?"

"Yes, or so it would seem." She took the jar back and unscrewed the lid, and without giving it too much thought, took Brennan's hand again and tipped some into it.

"Squeeze it. Still just dirt?"

He closed his eyes and concentrated. Yes, but wait, something niggled, then something sent a shiver down his spine—a *ghost walking on his grave*, his granny would have said.

"What's in that, something from a toxic waste dump? It gave me shivers."-He was busy shedding all traces from his hand back into the jar.

Ah, so he had some sensitivity himself, thought Maddy. Not the intensity of her own, but enough that it could help with understanding.

"Not a waste dump, no, at least not in our modern terms, but toxic, yes, maybe, probably, at least on one level." She tightened the lid and set it down on the step below.

"Let me tell you a story." She wrapped the shawl more tightly around her shoulders. Bren reached over to hold her close, and she tucked in easily right under his arm, a comforting warmth to keep the chill of the night away, she thought, and the chill buried in the jar.

She told him, first, of her intrinsic ability to sense or 'see' things, and how it was not well received by her mum or her mum's boyfriends. She had no idea who her real da was, or if any of her ancestors had the sight as well. She clutched the shawl tighter as her mind traveled that distant road again. There came a day when her mum had had enough and Maddy had suddenly been uprooted and relegated to the country with her Gran. That had been twenty years ago, when she was eight.

"I remember it clearly. I was scared, not an unusual feeling back then, but this was more, the suddenness, the frantic tossing of clothes, no rhyme or reason but simply whatever came to hand and then the fury emanating from the front seat of the borrowed car." Maddy paused, took a calming breath.

"I'd not been in a car much. To move, yeah, but in the city and sometimes just a few blocks away. I'd never been out of the city. Knew nothing of the vast green, the cows, the sheep. I remember my hands, wet with sweat and shaking with fear holding tight on the vinyl seat covering. What was happening? Where were they going? Frannie, my mum, turned in the driver's seat, hard eyes pinning me to the back seat like a bug on a board. 'Ye're nothing but trouble,' she said, turning her head back to watch the road. 'Best to be trouble where no one will be bothered by it. So stay quiet and mind, I'll not have the old woman shipping ye back.'"

She carefully picked the jar up and turned it around and around in her hand. Then set it aside again.

"So here I stayed, and after a while I flourished. Gran accepted me, as simple as that, and loved unconditionally. She taught me how to adapt my abilities to sense or see things. How to navigate without making waves."

Maddy then relayed the visit from her Gran's friend, Belinda O'Neill, and the concern for her prize roses. They both had a laugh over the old codger chatting up Belinda's Rose Award competitor, and how now Belinda was going to apologize to the woman for mistaking her for a dog.

"But Bren, there is something else there, something deeper and more... maybe tinged with evil—I think even you felt it, yeah?"

"Yeah, I suppose." He flexed his fingers, watched his hand open and shut, as he remembered the tingling sensation he'd gotten. "I've not the sight you do, but it did feel, well, odd, is the only way I can describe it. Do you feel it, or do you see it?" Bren's curiosity had been piqued. He hadn't really taken in the reality of being with someone who connects to, what, spirits? History? Old energy some might say. And what did she feel when she touched him? Could she 'read' him? Was he really ready for that?

"A bit of both. The visions at the stones? Those were unusually strong and intense and are rare." She wrinkled her brow. "In fact, I think those were the most turbulent and unexpected I've ever had." She shook it off, as if shedding the memory. "Some come as dreams that I know are related to something I've touched or been close to, and sometimes, just as you say, a niggly feeling that I have learned to listen to." A moment of quiet settled between them. "I think lots of folks get those, and dismiss them, then say they knew something was going to happen, you know."

Maddy pulled her shawl in closer. "I had visions, dreams if you will, the night after Mrs. O'Neill left the jar with me. I've been trying to reconcile what I remember of those dreams with what I felt at the stones. It was powerful and dark, what I felt when I touched that stone. You saw that." She stopped for a moment, pleating the edges of her shawl. "I'm sorry

I left, sorry I ran. I was fueled by old fears, visions of terror, darkness and embarrassment coupled with surprise. It all took over." She stopped her fidgeting. "I know there is a connection between what I felt there and what I sense from this jar, just not the how or the why. I think, feel," she amended, venturing into shaky territory, "it has to do with a seal, a Selkie, and a person of some power or means, with dark intent, but nothing is clear, it's like a window you can't quite see through."

"Or a puzzle missing pieces?" Bren added.

Bren picked up the jar and looked at it. It was getting darker out now, and it was little more than a weight in his hand.

"Would it help to know if there is something actually in here that would give us clues to those missing pieces? I can have it analyzed in the lab at school. I wouldn't tell them why, or I could just tell them I am helping a friend with a garden and want to get on her good side with a soil analysis."

She bumped his shoulder at that. "You're already on my good side." She then realized he'd said "give *us* clues". He was with her on this then. He knew about her sight, treated it like it was no big deal, and he still wanted to be part of it, part of her. It was something she would need to get used to. Letting someone join in meant the good with the bad. Well, he'd seen the bad, she supposed he wouldn't object to seeing the good if it came to that.

"You're up for more, eh?"

"Maddy, whatever the 'more' brings I'm with you, and if the gods are willing, I'd still like to be with you after we figure it out. And we will figure it out; I don't need your sixth sense to know that."

She leaned into him, into his confidence and strength. "I truly am sorry I ran, I know it must have been a shock, almost as much as it was to me. It's just, well, it's been a road, you know, with bumps and heartache to come to terms with what I have inside me. To understand it as a bonus, not a defect." She sighed. "I was never that put out with you...no, ach, truth be told, I was, but I just had to have some time." She nodded towards the bag he'd brought out. "If that's a peace offering, though, I'll be having it now, if you please. As my wise Gran said, a woman always likes a gift."

He stretched his free arm down and grabbed the bag that had been tucked at his feet on the lower step.

"Let me turn on a light, shall I?"

Now

Bren stood, bag still in hand, found and flipped a switch just inside the door. Soft sconces glowed on either side of the red door. He sat back down on the top step, pulled Maddy back into his side.

Then he handed over the Bodelian bag. She felt all around the edges. A book, then. Carefully folding back the canvas straps, she pulled out the cloth-wrapped book.

"I see you went all out on the wrapping, professor."

"I get creative on short notice."

"I'll remember that."

She unfolded the dish towel, to reveal the treasure inside: an ancient herbal. "Bren, it's wonderful, it's too much…" Words failed her. It was perfect.

"Like it then, do you?" he said with a wry grin you could hear in his voice.

She carefully turned the pages of the old book. "Oh look, salves, possets and unguents, don't you just love that word?" She rolled it around again, accenting each syllable. "Un-gu-ents. And oh look, tinctures, teas…copperplates with hand coloring, what a treasure! Oh Bren, is it yours from a collection? Are you sure?"

He wasn't going to tell her it had been in his family for generations. "Yes and yes. I figure I know where it is if I ever have need of it. Just promise me I won't be your guinea pig for any of those potions." He pointed at the ancient writing and winced then he hugged her closer. "Now, should I take the jar, and see what an analysis says?"

She lifted the jar, stared at it then handed it over to him. "I wouldna think it could hurt, and may get us to a resolution sooner. I keep feeling like I'm missing something, or that there is something I need to do, some circle that needs closing." She sighed.

They sat together. A comfortable silence. Maddy had never experienced that with anyone except perhaps her Gran. Certainly not with a man. The few relationships she had tried were always fraught with anxiousness and a concerted effort to do and say the right thing to make it work. It made her think of what Bren had said about his ex-wife.

"I've not dated much, and never a long-term relationship. Too worried I suppose about reactions, about showing my true self inadvertently. I figured it would be me and Gran, and that was okay." She looked over at him. "But I do wonder if I'd been more confident, would one of those relationships have blossomed. Did I not trust enough?"

They sat quietly for a few minutes.

"Do you miss her at all, miss what you might have had together? Do you think if you'd only done something differently...?"

Bren knew she was thinking of Christine and his marriage.

"It wasn't so much that I could have been different, or done different, but I guess I wasn't as content with who I was, or knew exactly who I wanted to be. And given that, I suppose I just wasn't invested enough in the relationship. Some of that comes from maturity. I have a much better sense of who I am now. I think that makes a huge difference when you are completing a picture, making two into a whole. It's not that you can't stand on your own, mind, but that you are better with the person who's right. They make you better, and in turn you make them better."

"Yeah, I can see that. I tried to be someone I wasn't when it came to relationships. My mum wasn't the best role model, as you've probably guessed, and then, too, what I have in me. Not many men are ready for that, not many women, either, truth be told."

Maddy stifled a yawn. "Sorry, it's been a busy couple of days."

"Yes, and then some," replied Bren. He paused, needing to ask, to tell. What she had in her, it was a vital part of who she was, and he wanted to understand, to support and show her he accepted. Yes, startling and rare, but somehow intriguing and more than a bit special.

"Maddy, what you went through at the stones, and I've no need to know right now, we'll get to that if and when we need, but it must wear your body and mind out something fierce. I can't say I won't react again, but I hope, if there is a next time, it will be in support of you, not scaring the both of us."

"I know. Sometimes it scares me too." She left it at that and yawned again.

Bren stood and reached down to give her a hand up. "It's bedtime, love, and I've a drive home and a summer intern to meet in the morning."

"Let me just go in and get your leftovers." Maddy said as she quickly stepped through the door and to the kitchen. It didn't take but less than a minute and she was back, tucking the containers into the Bodelian bag. "A few minutes in the microwave with a cover open slightly and you'll be all set."

"Thank you for a lovely evening. I've meetings most of tomorrow, but maybe we can try another picnic one day this week. This time without historic stones."

"Yes, I'd like that. You'll text me when you are home okay?"

"Ah, already a nag." He sighed and shook his head. Maddy knew he was joking. "Yes, I'll try to remember."

Her hand was warm on his arm. With his free hand—the other was holding the precious jar of dirt—he tipped her chin up. An eyebrow raised in question, a lock of his hair tumbling over the other eyebrow... She gave a slight nod, then he kissed her.

He pulled away slightly to see her expression—her eyes were closed and there was just the hint of a smile. He reached for the Bodelian bag she'd been holding. "Don't want to forget this."

Her eyes popped open at that and stared at the bag in her hand.

"Oh, no, of course not." She was all flustered. Brennan was acting so normal about all of this. Maybe she was making it into more than it needed to be. Her heart winced at that. Was she mistaken? Then she took a good look at him as she handed over the bag, and put her hand on his left arm-she could feel the energy vibrating under his skin. Ah, not so mistaken then. Finding a bold streak she never knew she had, she stepped up on tip toes, put her hand on the back of his head, pulled him down and kissed him again.

"Ah, Maddy love, do you know what you do to me? I hate to go, but its leave now or not at all, and I am pretty sure your Gran would rethink her good assessment of my character if we were still sitting together here on the porch or at the breakfast table in the morning."

"A gentleman to the core. Yes, Gran is remarkably modern to a point, but I'm quite sure not on that particular point." Maddy gave him one last hug, and walked with him to his Rover.

He opened the door, set the bag and jar carefully on the passenger seat.

"I'll take good care of the mysterious dirt and get it to the lab as soon as I can."

He climbed in, shutting the solid door with a thud. With a turn of the key and a flick of the lights he was lost in the glare. He waved out the window as he backed up, then was gone in the fog.

It was eerily quiet given how her life had just shifted. The stars would still be shining just above the light fog, the sun would rise in the morning, the tides would come and go and yet, in her world, nothing would be the same again.

NOW

The interrogations began first thing the next morning—same gist, different rooms, different towns. Maddy's was in person, with Gran across the breakfast table, and Bren, in his flat, with his phone to his ear.

Maddy hid a smile as she imagined what her dear Gran would be sputtering about if Brennan had indeed still been there in the morning. Maddy found she wasn't opposed to it, and decided right then and there to look into being prepared. Her Gran, however, would take some careful diplomacy and maneuvering. Bren had not said a word about commitments to each other. Maddy herself wasn't ready to make that leap yet but maybe more ready than Bren, who had been through it once, even if it was a while ago. His feet may still tingle with cold at the thought of signing up again.

"Maddy, dear girl, did ye hear me then? Is your head in the clouds this morning?" Gran rapped her spoon against her teacup, emphasizing her inattentiveness.

"Of course, Gran. You wanted to know how it all went with my 'professor fella.'"

"Well, don't keep an old woman waiting; I don't have that kind of time to spare at my age."

"Gran, I am sure you'll live to be a hundred or more, but I'll tell you. Now, listen."

"Well sure, and isn't that exactly what I have been trying to do!"

"We both apologized for our parts and then had a chat about this and that." Maddy knew her Gran was itching for more.

"And just what kind of this and that would that be?" the older woman boldly wanted to know.

Maddy just smiled and took a sip of her coffee and a last bite of her toast. "*This* would be my business and *that* would be none of yours," she said, smiling. Then to soften the retort, leaned over and kissed her. "But I will say that all is well, thank you very much, and we'll be seein' each other again. Now,

I've work to do, and I believe Irene Connelly is coming soon to pick you up for the Church Charity committee meeting." Maddy rose to take her dishes to the sink, a smile on her lips when her Gran couldn't see. The old woman was as dear to her as anything, but Maddy was afraid that if she gave her Gran slack in the line and let her meddle even more, she would take that line and Brennan would be tied, trussed and at the altar saying 'I do' in no time flat. Best she held that line right and tight to the mooring post sooner than later.

Erin called just as Bren had turned off his alarm and rolled over, hoping for just a few more minutes of sleep. The day had caught up with him, and he was more than ready for bed by the time he'd reached home. It had been foggy most of the way and slow going in spots, but he'd been wound up, and when he finally hit his bed, found sleep to be elusive.

A glance at his phone confirmed it was the inevitable call from his sister. She'd not relent, he knew well, so it was best to get it over with.

"Yeah," he growled out.

"Aren't you awake yet, Bren? I've been up for ages now and on my second cup of coffee."

Bren groaned at that. "Good, maybe you could just pour a wee bit in the phone then for your sorry brother."

"Sorry, is it? It didn't go well?" Erin sounded concerned and a bit surprised.

"No, it went fine, in fact more than fine." Bren sat up and stretched one arm, switched the phone over and then stretched the other arm. "We're to get together again later this week for another picnic—no ancient stones this time, or ancient anything, I promised."

He got up and headed straight for the kitchen. The phone to his ear with one hand, he grabbed the electric kettle with his other hand, filled it, set it on its stand and turned it on. The cafetiere was already loaded up with coffee grounds, an evening habit that started in graduate school when he'd had to make the dash to early morning classes.

"Ah, grand. I knew you had it in you to make a go of it. What's her house like?" Erin asked.

Why did women always want to know these things? A nesting instinct he supposed. Maybe that wasn't politically correct thinking these days, though, so he wisely kept his mouth shut on that score. The kettle was just starting to gurgle and hiss as he reached into the fridge for butter and jam to slather on a stale crumpet.

"Small stone cottage with a front porch and red door. In Kinnvere, not too far from the coast. Nice gardens, trim and traditional, like her Gran."

"The infamous Grandmother. She liked you then?"

"Yes, I've been invited back anytime."

"And you liked her?"

"She's no one's fool. Old fashioned about a lot of things, but knows the score and isn't afraid to speak her mind. Maddy came to live with her when she was only eight—can you imagine being sent off to live with Granny Blaisdel when you were in, what, third grade?"

"Where were her parents?"

"Not there for her, for sure. No da around, and her mum and her mum's various boyfriends couldn't deal with her knowing things. Things that hadn't happened yet. If you get my drift."

"Ah, like Aunt Aggie, saying she had 'the sight'. And I believed her." Erin paused, chuckling at the memory. "Until I caught her with a shot glass and her ear up to a closed door." Aunt Aggie was only one of a bushel of odd relatives that were to be found on their family tree. "But with Maddy it's not a glass and a good ear is it? She's truly gifted?"

"Yeah, she is." Bren was still wrapping his head around it, but he believed her without question. He'd seen what had happened at the stones, and had no doubt she'd felt and seen something extraordinary. Which made her extraordinary.

"But her mother didn't see it as a gift. It was a burden, and a bother. Apparently she explained dumping her with her Gran as 'Ye're trouble enough, best to be trouble in the country where no one will mind' and that was that." He felt a bit guilty about sharing Maddy's family history with Erin without asking Maddy first, but hey, this was his sister, and he knew she would respect it.

"Well, if her mum's such an eejit than maybe 'twasn't such a bad thing."

"No, I agree with you there, and so would Maddy now. Her Gran did a fine job raising her."

"So when do we get to meet her?"

"Soon. It's early days yet Er, let me ease her into the whole family thing. She's used to just herself and her Gran and they live pretty quietly. I don't want to be scaring her off when I just got her back."

THEN

Alfred, Esthwyn and Gwain's eldest, was working in the yard, fixing sisal fish netting when he heard the distinct clomp and stomp of large horses. His hands stilled and gripped the rough rope. *The Abbot's guards.* There was only one reason, he could imagine, to explain their more frequent travels down this road. The road that went by his family's holdings and then Moira and Ula's croft. He'd heard the rumors, the concern for the young woman whom Moira had sheltered and taken in as family. The whispers among the fishermen and villagers about the Abbot's interest. There were furtive glances, shudders and crossing of hands over head and hearts to ask God to bless and protect, because catching the Abbot's eye in such a way was not considered a blessing. Moira was well liked, and so was Ula. Alfred had only recently accepted his own feelings for the young woman. His interest had grown from fascination and friendship, then into admiration and taken root.

In quiet moments out fishing, or like now, when mending, tending, he'd think of her, of what she might be doing, of how he could finagle an encounter. Sometimes, when Moira needed help, he'd have a chance to speak with Ula. They'd started out simply—a nod here, a word there. It had expanded into longer conversations. Laughing over his siblings' antics, or Ula's disasters at cooking.

He'd not shared his feelings yet with the young woman. There was something he couldn't quite pinpoint, something that still felt innocent and naive about her. *Time*, he thought, *give her a bit more time*. They were both young yet. He had no idea of Ula's age, exactly, but living with three younger sisters gave him a good gauge. Maybe close to Elyn's age, his oldest sister who was a couple of years younger than himself. His thoughts came back to the here and now as the horses continued past their gate and down the road. What if she was alone? Or even if Moira was home, the woman was old. Sturdy and capable, but old. Suddenly the netting was set aside as he bolted out the gate and down the road.

Ula shivered. Those strange chain-clad men who paused at their gate made her afraid. Moira had taught her to stand still and be calm when she was afraid, like when the ram faced her down, or if the heavens thundered and sparked. When they left, she went to sit down on the bench just outside their door, and took deep, even breaths. The sky was still blue, the clouds still white, the sheep quietly grazing in the pasture beyond their little yard. Moira was out checking the fencing and would be back soon.

Then she heard the rumble and tumble of running footsteps on the road, and she stood quickly to see who it was. Should she hide? Ah, 'twas only Alfred, running so fast down the road that his legs seemed to propel him forward faster than his body could keep up with. He was all spinning arms and spinning legs. She felt a laugh bubbling up, but then he came bursting in through the gate, surprising her with his urgency. Was something amiss with one of his family?

"Ula, Ula, are ye okay then? Did they scare ye, did they talk to ye?" He bent over, his hands on his knees, catching his breath.

She looked at him curiously. She had been afraid, but why would he be concerned or think her to be more scared or worried if they'd spoken?

He saw her confusion and tried to explain his abrupt arrival.

"I saw the Abbot's guards go by and followed. I can see by the way the dirt is stirred that they stopped here at your gate."

Ula had a hard time understanding why a man always had to explain the obvious.

"Thank ye, Alfred. I am fine, as you can see. They did scare me a bit, but I was still and..." what was the word... "respectful. They left."

"The next time, come get me."

Now, she thought to herself, how practical was that? He might be fishing—and what was she to say to those imposing guards? *Excuse me, you can wait here but I must leave to go find Alfred?* She furrowed her brow. And did he really think there would be a "next time"?

Alfred saw her frown, and thought she was worried about bothering him.

"I mean it, Ula. They may answer to the Abbot, but I am not sure they have pure hearts or noble intentions." That was as much as he dare say.

She thought it wise to simply agree with him. "Yes, Alfred, if I'm afraid I will let you know. Now, how is your family?" Ula tried to steer the conversation to safer shoals.

"Young Ian is into everything, and the girls love him and hate him all at once, but we're faring right fine, ye know. The fishing has been good, the weather fine, and we've paid the tithe for the year. Ma will rest easier she says knowing we'll all go to heaven."

Ula nodded. This idea of having to give your hard-earned goods for something as ethereal and incomprehensible, to her at least, was difficult to understand. Moira had tried to explain it to her, but it still made no sense. Especially given the mistrust so many had in the motives of that eerie Abbot. She had passed him once when she and Moira were walking the road along the coast, and caught him staring right at her with a look that gave her shivers.

Moira had noticed that lingering look as well, and on their way home from market, out of hearing distance of any of the Abbot's many spies told Ula, "I don't like the look the Abbot has on ye. He may just be curious, but I've a feeling in my bones 'tis more than that. Ye'll be careful now, will ye?"

Ula promised she would be watchful. There was plenty to keep her busy right there around the croft, so she rarely went into town, and if she did it was always with Moira by her side. The only time she was out alone was when she went down to the shore in the wee small hours of the morning to retrieve her seal self from the cave and immerse herself once again in sea water for nourishment and frolic. The call of the ocean had become more distant over the years, but like an addiction, it would slowly bloom inside of her until she had to answer. Moira understood and gave her safe blessings on each journey. The older woman seemed to sense when the pull was growing inside her, when she could not ignore the call of her bones, when her very life blood needed the salt of the sea.

When Moira would see the young woman lifting her head to catch a whiff of the salt air on the wind, or stare into the distance towards the ocean, she would say, "Go, my child, go. It is what you need. It is still a part of you, who you are, who you are going to be. Be one with it, and nourish that part of your soul. Without it, well, you would live, but it would be like me losing an arm or a leg—you wouldn't be whole, you wouldn't be able to be all you can be. It is like when I lost Hugh. I am still here, and the gods have blessed me with you, but I miss Hugh, and what we had together. There is yet a part of me that will always be missing. Be safe, be vigilant, be home soon." Then Moria would kiss her forehead and bless her.

Alfred was heading out fishing with his father particularly early one morning, in the cove near their croft. Through the mist he thought he saw movement on the beach. He knew that gait, that swing of hair. Was that Ula on the beach? He worried about her out so early and by herself. He looked again and she was gone. *Must be the mist playing tricks*, he thought. But soon after, he saw a seal in the water near their boat watching him. It wasn't unusual to see seals along the West Coast, but this one had a look about the eyes. A look that lingered, a look that seemed familiar, and that somehow seemed more knowing than others, somehow more human.

Alfred worked hard beside his father, checking the nets, pulling in fish as needed, sorting, tossing, cleaning. There were times when there would be an extended lull, and his mind would wander. In one of those rare moments of calm, he turned over and over in his mind the seal sighting and seeing Ula so early on the shore. She loved fish, she sometimes seemed a bit lost, and although she had been living now with their old neighbor for many years, it was never fully clear how she got there and where she had come from. Found on the beach, they'd said. As a younger boy he didn't care, really, after the notion of a shipwreck was dismissed. Beyond that he'd paid little to no attention to the new neighbor, but as he matured, and as his attraction to Ula grew, he began to wonder a bit more about her.

He was no stranger to the myths and legends of his culture. Although the idea that Ula could be a Selkie seemed preposterous at first, he couldn't quite shake its hold on his imagination. How to ask? How to find out? Did it, or would it make a difference? As a young lad, he would have just accepted, but as a maturing young man, he questioned. His father always said honesty was best. Maybe he could find a way to ask Ula directly. With this mostly settled in his mind, he went back to checking old nets for loose spots, watching the wind and keeping an eye on the blue expanse all around for signs of a school of fish, or perhaps a watchful seal.

NOW

Brennan and Maddy's plan to have another picnic was perfect, except for the sudden torrential rain that had them scrambling to gather it all up, throwing it in Bren's Rover, and relocating to his kitchen table. They had arrived at his flat drenched, laughing, and despite the soaking, thoroughly enjoying themselves.

Maddy felt a bit scandalous in one of Bren's tee shirts and nothing else but her underthings, yet somehow was totally comfortable. He had changed into sweats, but had yet to put on a shirt. This was fine in Maddy's opinion—he certainly wasn't hard on the eyes! The contents of the hastily repacked cooler were spread on the simple plank table.

Maddy tipped her bottle of brew.

"Here's to a fine day despite mother nature." She clinked her bottle with his.

"I'll echo that," Bren replied.

Maddy took a long swig, set the bottle down on the table, and looked squarely at the man who had slipped into her life unexpectedly, had her looking towards a future she hadn't even imagined a month ago. Simple steps: a tumbled rose bush, then a jar of dirt, an inquiring email, and suddenly she was on a journey that led to a milestone in her life.

"Bren, why are ye not skeptical or afraid of me? Of what I am?" She took up the bottle and had another drink to hide her sudden fear of his answer, her innate nervousness about the subject.

"Afraid of you? You are as soft as pudding. Just as sweet, too," he quipped as he rummaged through the offerings on the table. Then he looked up and saw the serious look she was sending him.

He reached over and tipped up her chin, looking directly into her eyes, rubbing his thumb on her cheek. "There is nothing, and I repeat, nothing to be afraid of. You were given a very special gift. An artist sees the world in one way, and is able to put it on canvas, a writer on paper, a craftsman or builder with wood, a composer with music. Why be afraid of Bach, or Mozart, or Da Vinci for that matter? What you have may not be seen by others, but neither were the Brandenburg concertos heard until Bach heard them in his mind and put the notes on paper, or the Eiffel tower imagined by anyone other than Eiffel. Your mother and her kind are not afraid of you, they're afraid of what you may see about them."

Her eyes teared, and she tried hard to keep them from spilling over. She took his hand and squeezed it, then leaned over to kiss him.

"And what of your family? Will they feel the same?"

"Ah, let me tell you about my Great-Great Aunt Cleona, on my Da's side. It's said she lived in the east wing of the manor, never married, and as family lore has it, regularly turned into an owl at night. It seems the barn cats had to be fed extra as Aunt Cleona took care of all the rodents on the property for as long as she lived. I think she died at 102."

Maddy took another swig, and laughed, pointing her bottle at him.

"Really? Are you making it up now to make me feel better?"

Bren shook his head and laid his hand on his heart.

"No, God's honest truth. You can ask them about her when you meet."

"Do you think changelings might run in the family?" she asked with a grin.

"I've never heard tell of any others, but you never know. Our family tree is lousy with mysteries, secrets and odd lots," he quipped back with a sly grin of his own.

"Speaking of mysteries, any luck with the lab? Was your friend willing to take a look at the dirt for clues?" Maddy asked.

"Peter was happy to help. I took the jar over a few days ago and let him know my future depended on careful reading of the contents." Bren took a bite of his sandwich. "He's on a bit of a lull with the students mostly gone for the summer break, so he should be able to get back to me soon. His antennas are up and quivering, wondering who's the woman who has me so intrigued. Says he's eager to meet you."

Maddy looked a bit startled at that. What did he tell his friend?

"I didn't tell him any details, just that I was hoping to score with a gorgeous gardener and needed to know a soil analysis."

"Such flattery, Professor O'Connor. I've no wonder all your female students swoon at your feet. I saw that young waitress in the pub eyeing you. One of your students I would guess."

"Yeah, Sinead, majoring in Arts, and took my class on Myth and Culture. I wouldn't say eyeing so much as curious about the mysterious woman that caught her professor's attention. I haven't dated all that much since I took on the Professorship. I am sure she was texting all her mates behind the bar right quick after she served us. Word is out. Thankfully it's summer break and we'll be among the deleted, or at least in the text abyss on her phone well before term starts again."

"Hmm, trendy today, deleted tomorrow? Hard to keep up with the younger set, isn't it? So, back to the analysis. Your mate gives us a list of ingredients so to speak, and then what? I've been wondering what I'd, no *we'd*," she amended, remembering he was in it with her, "do with the information"

"I've been thinking on that as well. I suppose it depends on what he finds. I'm thinking though, have you made a list of your visions, your impressions? Maybe seeing it on paper will show a pattern or a direction we can track, like footprints?"

"Hmm, I hadn't thought of it that way. I can, yes, certainly, see what I can remember. So much is fleeting and emotional, not clear pictures."

"Even a list of images, or how you felt would be a good. Would it help to close your eyes and rattle off what you think of? I can jot it down. Or dare I mention going back to the standing stones?" He took her hand, squeezed. "You wouldn't need to touch them—maybe just being close, and knowing what there was, will bring something to mind. This time I'd be with you and better prepared for whatever comes your way." Bren kept his hand in hers. "I know it takes its toll on you, but you'll be prepared this time as well, and I'll be with you one hundred and ten percent."

"Aye, and that's a great comfort to me, Bren." She squeezed his hand, leaned over and kissed him.

The remnants of the indoor picnic were spread over the wide plank table. Maddy stood and started to gather the plates and cups.

"I'll wash, you dry?" She winked at him. The plates and the cups were paper.

Bren followed her into his kitchen, showed her where the bins for trash and recycling were hidden under the sink, then spun her around by the shoulders and held her tight. Her head fit perfectly on his shoulder. Despite the rain outside, she smelled of sun and the sea.

Maddy sighed deeply and settled in. They fit so well together in so many ways. She never knew a relationship could be like this. All her relationship experiences, her own few and watching her mother's multitude of disasters one after the other, were no match for the real thing. She didn't need the sight to know Bren was the one, for a lifetime if he would have her. That train of thought would need to wait, though.

She pulled gently away. "I'd best be heading home soon."

She started walking towards the pantry. The washer and dryer were stacked in a corner behind a folding door. Bren had thrown their damp clothes in the dryer when they first got home. Maddy pulled her dry clothes out and proceeded to change.

Bren watched her and groaned. "Let's plan another outing in the rain, and tell that sweet Gran of yours that you have an invite to spend the night with friend." He shook his head. "Ach, don't mind me. I'll not have you lie to your Gran. It's just... well it's just that... well, you know." Bren was seldom at a loss for words, but it seemed this woman tied his tongue like no other.

"I do know," she said with a sly grin, "and it will be all the sweeter when the time is right." Maddy had never been this bold with any of her previous relationships. Whether it was her insight or just plain and simple loving the right person, there was no sense in rushing what was sure to be a very pleasant and enjoyable courtship.

THEN

From his top floor window of the monastery, the Abbot watched the activity below and then gazed beyond to the village, the farms and hills. There were changes afoot in the hierarchy. Word had come that the old Bishop had fatally succumbed to a festering wound. His position was vacant until a new Bishop was elected. He was confident that the coveted position would be his and that he would soon be the sole arbiter and shepherd for lost sheep in his flock. That power was his destiny, as were the fruits of that power, those fruits ripe and ready for his plucking. He believed that God provided for those who were deemed worthy, who led the battle for those poor souls to gain enlightenment and a promised path to heaven.

A good warrior knew his enemies as well. Myth, pagan Gods, magiks. Stories and beliefs older than anyone could remember were passed down, were still whispered, worshipped. He devoted himself to wiping that slate clean, to banish any inkling of action or thought antithetical to the doctrine of the Holy Church. There could only be One Authority, one God who provided or punished according to deeds and devotion, and he saw himself as the appointed voice of that God.

And yet, the mysterious called to him, the ethereal rarity and otherworldly nature of the girl child, if she was indeed as some believed. His spies were everywhere and had passed along the whispers, the knowledge and acceptance of a creature beyond the Church's dictates and doctrines. Indeed, beyond the dictates and understanding of what it meant to be human, to be made in God's image. It was unnatural, and yet...

Hadn't he seen her himself as he'd walked the narrow cliff road? This fey creature who had eased into life with the widow woman. He learned she was called Ula, Jewel of the Sea. Yes, it was indeed a fitting name for this girl child, this Selkie, if the whispers rang true.

For months now, he'd had his guards watch her, openly and secretly. They reported only to him, and any questions or hint of gossip among them were dealt with swiftly and permanently. As time went on, he was convinced that she was meant to be his, sent to him and him only, by God, he'd told himself, to purify, to set on a Christian path, to make her repent and forgo her connections to any magiks, anything unworldly, unholy. And, in private moments, dark of night moments, he cherished the thought that she would be his, the rarest of jewels to be added to his collection of treasures.

The Abbot's guards approached his private chamber with caution. They had what he had asked for. It defied belief when they were given their orders. Had the old man gone mad? Muiredoch, the head guard, was paid well for his loyalty and silence, but even this request had him wondering if his life was worth coming up empty-handed. He'd been prepared to skin a seal just to satisfy the old man. But, amid much astonishment and bravado—although Muiredoch did see a few of his men cross themselves in prayer—they'd found the pelt in a sea cave.

Now he needn't worry; a reward was most certainly in the offing, and not just a heavenly one. The Abbot had promised to send Elspeth, the new laundry maid, up to his chamber with his payment if he succeeded. It looked like the comely young maid and a bag of gold were both to be his tonight.

NOW

They had snagged the corner table by the window, the one they had first sat at when they met. It had become one of their favorite places. Papers were spread out between the empty platter, Bren's pint glass and Maddy's tea.

She had spent the last several nights filling pages and pages of her notebook with descriptions and impressions. Two heads, one auburn and the other deep chestnut, were now bent over those pages with pencils in hand, circling and transferring ideas to a larger sheet of paper.

A young blonde woman passed by their table with an iced take-away drink in hand. "Maddy, what a surprise to see you here."

"Maureen, what a surprise to see *you* here. What brings you to Galway?" She saw Maureen looking over to Bren. "Let me introduce you. Professor Brennan O'Connor, this is Maureen Garraty, the owner of the Sea and Soul gift shop. She very kindly takes on my soaps, herbs and bread to sell."

Bren stood up slightly and reached out a hand. "Please, call me Bren."

"Maddy, I can see you will need to come in very soon to restock my shelves and bring me up to date," Maureen said with a noticeable twinkle and raised eyebrow, a clear sign they needed to talk. She turned to Bren. "A great pleasure to meet you. Maddy is too modest, though, her goods always sell out. A real hit with tourists and locals alike. Seems she has a knack for having just the right thing for me to have on the shelf when a customer comes in with a special need."

Maureen was one of the few friends who knew of Maddy's ability to intuit or see what others might not. The woman was canny, Maddy had to give her that, and had cornered her one day in the tiny storeroom of her shop and with hands on hips wanting to know just how it was that Maddy seemed to have right to hand, more often than not, what odd thing a customer might come in and ask for. Maddy had hemmed and hawed, then under Maureen's penetrating gaze, given in and blurted out the whole story. Maddy remembered clearly being ready to pack up all her goods and flee, but what did Maureen do, but reach over and give her the biggest hug. "Is that all, then?" she'd said. Then she went on to say it was sure a boon to her, and Maddy as well, as the customers went away happy. *Happy customers, happy bank account*, Maureen had announced with a high five. The friendship grew and blossomed. Now, Maddy looked closely at her friend, trying not to pry.

"So, you've not said what brings you to Galway in the middle of a work day? Is everything okay?" Maddy asked. Maureen was just a few months pregnant with their first child.

"Ah, doctor's appointment at the hospital."

"Old Doc McVinney couldn't see you?" Maddy was worried now. Doc McVinney was the local GP and saw everyone in town. He was clever, kind, and very competent.

"It was Doc McVinney who set up the appointment." Maureen took a deep breath. "An ultrasound, for the babe. He says I'm farther along than he originally thought, and it seems to be standard practice now to check things out a few months in anyway. Sean had a business appointment in Galway. We agreed to meet at the hospital so he'll be there too."

Maddy raised her hand close to Maureen's belly. "May I?"

"Of course," Maureen said without hesitation.

Maddy gently laid her hand on Maureen's expanding middle.

"Ah," Maddy said as she gently pulled her hand away and picked up her pencil.

"And...? You can't just leave it at that now." Maureen gripped Maddy's shoulder with her free hand. "Everything's all right? I feel fine, but Maddy did you sense...?" Maddy's friend looked pointedly at Bren.

"It's okay Maureen, he knows and he's good with it." Maddy smiled at Bren.

Maureen stepped around the table and gave Brennan a hug. "It's nice to know there are still some smart men around. She's worth her weight in gold and then some, and don't you go forgettin' that or you'll be dealin' with the likes of me." She laughed when she said it, but Bren knew she was serious. He was just glad she had friends watching out for her, and said as much.

"He's a keeper, this one, my girl." Maureen grinned at Maddy while pointing at Bren. "So," turning her attention and her finger to Maddy, "what did you feel?"

Maddy tapped her pencil a couple of times on the table. She didn't want to spoil the results of the ultrasound, but her friend would worry if she didn't tell her what she felt.

"Okay, this isn't official, but I think medical science will back me up on this one. Are there any twins in your family or Sean's family?"

Maureen went ashen. Maddy quickly stood up, took the drink from her friends hand, put it down on the table and gave her a steadying hug.

"You're okay with it? I'd not meant to give you a scare."

"Oh no, Maddy, it's wonderful, but a bit of a surprise, yeah. I need to wrap my head around it. Wait until Sean hears. I bet he'll take credit for being very clever getting a two for one deal?" Sean was a local real estate agent, she explained to Bren, and always wheeling and dealing. All three of them laughed at that.

"God save me if it's two boys with Sean's energy." Maureen looked right at her friend. Maddy simply shook her head. "My lips are sealed. Let the nurse have some surprises yet to share."

"Okay, be that way." She shrugged her shoulders. "Don't worry, I'll let the ultrasound nurse do her job and act surprised with the 'double the trouble' results," she said with a chuckle. "Can't take all their fun away, now can I? I'll call later tonight, yeah?" Maureen gave her friend another hug. Maddy sat back down.

Maureen looked up at the Goodness of Guinness clock on the wall. "I'd best be on my way. Don't want to be late for the big news." She walked away towards the door, and Maddy and Bren could see her shaking her head, hand on her belly and muttering, "twins, oh my..."

"Twins, eh? She'll have her hands full." Bren watched as the heavy oak door shut.

"Nothing she can't handle. She comes from a big family, and she's juggled owning a store with a busy husband for years. I've no doubt she will take this in stride and have them all well in hand even before they are born." Maddy smiled as she thought of the good friends she had made in this corner of Ireland. There was a time when she felt alone and lost without her mum, even as bad as that home life was, because it was all she knew. Now she could only thank the fates that sent her to her Gran's, and now the fates that had her meeting Brennan. She looked over and smiled at him just as he turned to look at her.

"What is running through your mind now? Or dare I ask?"

"Not anything like that... just how grateful I am that a jar of dirt landed me in your lap, so to speak."

"I wouldn't mind having *you* in my lap, but maybe we'll save that for later, yeah?" Bren smiled and winked at her, laying his hand on her cheek for the briefest moment.

"Now, I think we are getting somewhere, from the looks of things."

He turned back to the papers on the table. "Tell me what you see."

Maddy sat back and took a sip of her tea.

Bren finished the last of his pint, set the glass down and leaned back. "Well, you were originally thinking about a Selkie, who, as you know, as myth has it, is a creature born of the sea, but able to shed their skin on land and become human for a period of time." Leaning forward, he made another note on the paper and circled her word *Selkie*. "Add to that the marginalia I found in a 13th century manuscript purported to be from the monastery at

Kilneamh. There were depictions of a girl who is shown peering out of the round tower. And in the same section, pictures of seal-like creatures." He circled his notation, *marginalia*.

"Let's say a young female Selkie came ashore and caught the eye of someone. You had visions and dreams of the Selkie and then you felt the darkness and evil at the stones on a very personal level. If the two are connected, as we are thinking they are, then something happened to that Selkie girl. I'd say she was cut off from going home." He looked up at her, tapped his finger on the papers on the table. "Now it is a stretch, and it is thanks to you my Maddy, that I am even heading this direction, but maybe you, or we, are meant to help her go back, or by now her spirit, I suppose. I have no bloody idea what that means, or how we're to manage that I'll tell you, but it is the only answer I can see."

"Very perceptive of you, Professor, as I have come to the same conclusion. I'll give you an A+, with extra points for stretching your notion of what's possible by suggesting our task is to complete her circle and somehow return to her that which was lost." Maddy took another sip of her tea, pensively ran her finger over the circles on the paper in front of them. "So if that is the who, then we've only to figure out the how, the where, and the what."

They both stared at the table.

"When Gran is untangling a ball of yarn, she looks for the end, or the beginning, depending on how you look at it."

Brennan watched Maddy tap her lips and was thinking how soft and kissable they looked when she spoke up again.

"But where does the dirt come in? Any word from your lab chum?"

Bren jerked himself back to the pub, his heart racing as if caught in the headlights.

Maddy looked over at him, then smiled in an *I know what you were thinking* kind of way, then softly said "Later."

He cleared his throat, nodded, and smiled back. "Absolutely," was all he needed to say. "So, yeah, the lab stuff." Back to work.

"Peter sent me a text this morning. He's been unexpectedly busier than usual, as a summer TA broke his leg hiking and Peter's been filling in but promised he would have something for me by the weekend. I can bring the results over on Saturday afternoon if that works for you?"

"Gran would love it. She's been asking about you. Plan to stay for dinner?"

"And I'd love to see your Gran." He paused. "You know I'm only cozying up to you to get to see her." He twirled a loose curl around his finger, then Bren kissed her cheek. Anything more intimate would have to wait. "But you'll do for now."

"She's an easy one to love," replied Maddy

"She's not the only one easy to love." The words were out of his mouth before he even thought about it.

THEN

Love was not on the mind of the Abbot. Possession was. The girl would soon be his, to add to his collection of rare jewels and treasures. He stroked the soft fur, her fur. In a sense, he already held her captive—now to reel her in. It was just a matter of time. He closed his eyes and smiled. Just a matter of time.

Ula ran all the way home. It was gone. She couldn't quite comprehend it. Part of her was simply gone. She could no longer slip quietly into the sea, feel the saltwater surround her and flow through her fur. Her two legs on the solid earth felt leaden and clumsy. She tumbled over the threshold with more fear than grace. "Moira, Moira," the girl got out through her tears. "It's gone, I'm gone, I'm lost."

Her eyes wide and wet, she indeed looked lost. Moira had looked up from her mending as soon as she heard Ula's footsteps stumble through the doorway. The old woman got up as quickly as her aging bones would let her, opened her arms, and let the girl fold into her embrace.

"My child, my child," she crooned over and over. She wasn't going to tell her she'd be okay, because her life would never be the same again. Moira feared she knew where Ula's seal skin was, and feared more what it meant. Word had spread about the Abbot's guards venturing far afield, riding along the coast road, even wandering the beaches. Who knew they would go so far as to find and steal the link Ula had to the sea? She led the girl over to the bench by the fire pit and sat with her. Rocking back and forth, like the gentle swell of the ocean, calming, assuring.

Ula finally sat up, wiped her eyes with her shawl, and took a deep breath. "I will not be unhappy here, with you always. It is how you said, though... I am not quite whole. I will need to learn to adjust." She paused, looked up and away, thoughts gathering. "Ye know, Alfred has an old dog who lost his leg. He still manages to herd their sheep and do the job God had intended." Nodding to herself with resolve she turned, laid a hand on Moira's arm. "I'll stay always and be a comfort to you as you need."

"Ach, my dearest treasure, you are indeed my gift from the sea, but you are not to feel bound to me for the rest of my days. You will have a family of your own one day. It may not be the family you were born into, nor the family you may have imagined, but they will be a comfort to you. I look forward to that, for myself as well as for you."

Moira took Ula's hand and squeezed it. She had seen how Alfred looked at Ula, and recently how he had studied her harder and with more tenderness. It was a great contrast to how the Abbot had been looking at her. She would heartily welcome Alfred's intentions. The Abbot's were another matter altogether. It was no longer possible to put off the difficult talk she and her sweet girl from the sea must have.

"Ula, I think I know who has your seal self."

Ula looked up quickly with some surprise. "Ye do? We can get it?"

Moira shook her head and took Ula's hand once again. "Ye know how the Abbot and his guards have been watching you. How his guards have come down this road, even stopped and watched ye from the gate. The Abbot, he wants you, and not in a good nor kind way. Somehow he has discovered our secret, your secret, and sees you as a prize to add to his chest of gems, his curiosity cabinet of treasures, if you will. He is hoping to entice you to him by holding on to your seal skin. He has evil intentions, and I will make sure you are protected, but I can't make you a prisoner in your own home. It is exactly what the Abbot plans to do—make you his caged bird—and no one, animal nor human can nor should live like that." Moira paused, crossed herself and said quietly, as if the walls themselves had ears. "He is the devil's own. There's nothing Godly in the man t'all."

After a bit, she straightened, took a deep breath and looked straight at Ula. "I think we should let Alfred know. He can watch over ye better than I, or at least when I can't. Ye know he is quite fond of ye."

Ula realized that what had started as a simple friendship and neighborly kindness, she could see, now that she examined their relationship in this new light, that kindness and care had deepened over the years. She would trust Alfred with her life, and indeed it appeared that that was exactly what she needed to do.

One day slipped into the next. No sign of the Abbot, or his guards. Ula fed the sheep, swept the hearth, gathered the eggs, and watched for Alfred to come down the road. She was hoping the fates, or God, or some benevolent spirit would compel her dear friend to sense she needed to speak with him. It was hard enough to figure out exactly what she would say, but to go to him unbidden was just impossible to imagine.

A day, then two went by. Moira could see the young woman—and as events had progressed, she saw the girl had indeed become a young woman now—was watching up the road, and getting more and more skittish. She knew Ula did not feel confident enough to simply go next door and ask to speak with Alfred. Manners and deference were all well and good in their place, but this was not the time, nor the place, given the circumstances. The older woman finally decided to take matters into her own hands.

"Ula." The young woman looked up, startled. "I've need of some help fixing a loose board in the door in the barn. I think Alfred might be just the one to ask. Shall we go see if he is home?"

Ula smiled, nodded, and tucked her shawl under her arms, stood up and followed Moira out the door and up the road.

Alfred set his tools down and swung the barn door back and forth. "Just a loose nail," he said with a bit of puzzlement in his voice.

"Aye, 'twas as I thought. Easy to mend, then. Thank ye, Alfred," Moira said easily.

He turned and looked at his audience. Both of the women had been right behind him while he worked. It had only taken a few minutes, but Alfred had a feeling there was something he was missing here. It felt very much like when his sisters thought he was being thick-headed, or when they played a prank on him. The boy would have poked back at them, but the man he was becoming figured it was best to just ask for the truth. He put his hands on his hips. "Okay then, would ye mind tellin' me why it was ye had me come all ta way here to put one nail back into its place? Moira, ye've been managing without Hugh for years now, and I know ye've the tools." The young man scratched his head, shuffled his feet, then looked back up at women. "Sure'n

I'm glad to help ye, but is there somethin' else on yer mind then? And would ye be thinkin' to tell me now, or am I to stand here like an eejit and pull out guesses like fish from the sea 'til I'm old and withered?"

Ula looked at Moira, who shook her head and nodded towards Alfred. "Ye go on now, sit on the bench there by the door. It will be all right. I'll be just inside the barn if ye need me."

Moira looked over at Alfred then. "Ula has somethin' she's wantin' to tell ye now, young Alfred. I'll ask ye listen with an open heart and open mind." She turned then, and went to check on the new lambs.

"Ula?" asked Alfred

"Ah, come sit, Alfred." She gingerly sat herself on the wooden plank. "I need to tell ye somethin'."

"So Moira said."

"Yes, I suppose she did."

Moira could hear them from just inside the barn. Her heart ached to have them get on with it. Well, hopefully they would find their way soon enough. Like a young foal finding its legs for the first time; a bit uncertain, a bit wobbly at first, and next thing ye know, sure footed and confident.

When the older woman looked out at the two later, she could see Alfred's arm around Ula protectively, their heads close together and deep in conversation. She couldn't help but smile. Her Hugh often reminded her that bad things had a good side if you looked hard enough.

"I'll watch out for ye, Ula. Ye've no worry there." Alfred paused. He'd had his suspicions when he was younger, then as he'd grown, had left myth and mysteries behind. Now myth and miracle sat right beside him. He cleared his throat, ran a hand down her hair. "I grieve for what ye've lost, a part of yerself ye'll not ever have again."

Ula nodded. "I told Moira 'twas like your dog, Callum. He might only have the three legs now, but he manages and does his job and is no less for the loss. I will manage."

"To me, ye are certainly not less for the loss. Ye are still strong, and brave and the most beautiful woman I have ever known." He left it at that for the moment. Words were tumbling on his tongue, words of promise and the future, but those would wait for another time. She had enough to deal with, to adjust to. Ula looked back at him with a shy smile.

Alfred stopped by Moira's small croft late one afternoon, not long after he and Ula had had their talk. He and Ula had worked out a plan to try to keep her safe.

Ula was just shooing the hens into the barn for the evening. Alfred watched from the gate for a few minutes. It didn't matter to him the how or why of her existence. Whether through one God or many, he accepted that mysteries and miracles were a part of life. He was simply glad she was here. He felt in his pocket for the gift he hoped she would like. They'd come a long way, but he was still a bit nervous. He had talked to his own parents about his plans for the future, one in which Ula would have a major role. They didn't know the whole of it, but supported his vision completely, and were happy for their eldest son. Ula was well liked and would be welcomed into their family with open arms.

Ula looked up just then to see him. "Alfred." She smiled and her eyes lit up.

"Good eve to ye, Ula." He nodded and smiled himself. "I've a small gift for ye. Come sit, if ye will." Alfred nodded towards the bench by the door.

Ula made sure the clasp was snug on the hen's door, and made her way over to the doorway.

"I know ye miss the ocean fierce. I can see ye lookin' and catching the smell on the wind." He took Ula's hand. "I will do all in my power to find your seal self and make ye whole again."

"Alfred, no, it is too dangerous for ye. I'll not have ye put in harm's way for me. If indeed it is the Abbot..." She shuddered and shook her head. "No, ye must leave it be."

"Wheesht, ye're not to be thinking of that now. It will be as it will. I will be fine." He reached into the pocket of his jerkin. "I made ye this. Mayhap it will be some comfort, a part of the sea ye can wear until your other self is returned to ye." Alfred pulled out a necklace made of cowry shells and coral strung together and knotted on a leather cord.

NOW

"Vegetative nutrient rich organic matter and moss. In essence, peat," Maddy read aloud as she scanned the report Bren had handed to her. "That's not surprising. Belinda, Gran's friend," she added, "said she used peat for a secret fertilizer." She kept reading. "Shells, coral and some animal skin and fur fibers." Maddy set the paper down and looked over at Bren. "So that's what Peter found in the dirt?" Her astonishment ringing in her outburst. "I can see the peat, that makes perfect sense, but it's a stretch—literally and figuratively—for the shells and coral to be found so far from the shore and in a peat bog. I suppose, the fur could be from any wild animal." And, she thought to herself, could be further analyzed by a forensics lab.

They were sitting at Maddy's kitchen table with the remains of a pie, empty coffee cups, and of course, Peter's analysis. The lab report had no sooner been given to Bren, along with what was left of the dirt in the jar, when he phoned Maddy. She'd been in the middle of making pies. It wasn't a hardship in his book to set aside his schoolwork and offer to drive right out to her cottage, figuring he'd be getting a piece of that pie warm out of the oven. Seeing Maddy was a bonus anytime, but pie as well, that capped it right there.

"It's not impossible to imagine a prized collection of cowry shells or coral being carried by a pilgrim or traveler as small souvenirs from the ocean, but is the animal fiber relevant, or even concurrent with the shells? And how do they tie into our mystery? Shells and coral, buried so many miles from the sea? And the animal fibers? A wild animal, or even a pair of leather shoes, or clothing left behind or lost could have shed those. And so could a seal's skin be lost, but again, so far from the coast?" Maddy murmured, and rested her hand on her chin as she looked out beyond the window, out beyond the years to a time and place long gone.

So near and yet so very far away. She turned to focus on the here and now, on Bren, sitting so close she could feel the warmth of his body. One arm was draped over the back of her chair, his other hand combing through his unruly hair as he often did when thinking. Of course, this just made his hair even more of a muddle, which in Maddy's opinion made him all the more appealing.

"Well, Professor, what's your highly educated conclusion?" Maddy posed to him, turning in her chair while putting her feet up on the rung of his.

"I think you are right—could have been from a pilgrim or traveler with the shells and coral, and the fibers could be from clothing or shoes, but considering our particular..." he paused searching for the right word, "...interest, shall we say, then they must be connected to our Selkie in some way." He absently laid a hand on her knee. "It's the dirt that started it all and added to that you've gotten vibes from it, so to speak. So, let's say the seal fur fibers, if indeed they are, and coral and shells were somehow buried and preserved in a peat bog kilometers from the coast. Then, your Gran's friend digs some of it up and nourishes her rose bush with it." The jar of dirt sat quietly on the table alongside the empty dishes. Bren picked it up, turned it, stared at it then set it back down.

He scanned the report again and looked back up at her. "Nothing else in the report that leads me to think otherwise." He shook his head. "But, as you said, so far from the coast? That part just doesn't come clear."

"If only it could speak." Maddy said nodding in agreement and lifted the jar, staring at it as if she could will it to spout out answers. Turning it slowly in her hands, she realized that maybe it could speak, in a way. "What if we took the jar with us to the standing stones, or other random spots along the coast, or map a trail from the coast to the peat bog? The shells and coral would have had to travel about the same route, yeah? It's a long shot at best, but we may stumble on another clue, or I may have a feeling, a vision that will help."

He looked at her intently. *A 'vision', Jezus*, he thought and inwardly shivered. Then voiced his concern out loud. "I can't say it doesn't scare the bejesus out of me to think of you going through that again." He laid a hand on hers. "You know, what you did at the stones, it's etched in my memory. Still scares me spitless. But I'll be with you and they're not always that strong, yeah?"

Maddy smiled at him. "No, not always so powerful. That one was major, a nine on the Richter scale for sure. Like earthquakes," she explained. "Some are just tremors, while some, like that one, are total shake, rattle and roll." Maddy grinned. "I guess I shook, you got rattled, and then I rolled right out of there." They both laughed. It felt good to put it behind them like that. She got up and rummaged around in the drawer of the small table by the door.

Maddy seemed to take it all in stride. He wondered if he ever would.

"Aha, here." She opened up a neatly folded map and laid it out on the table over Peter's report. "It's a local road map of the West Country. Let's see if we can trace the most likely route. Perhaps you'll have a good notion of the old routes, pilgrimage routes. Am I right in thinking some of them would have been followed by modern roadways, just like old Roman roads are still used today?"

"Yes, certainly, geography played a role, and why bother carving out new paths when you can simply recycle the old?" Bren took a pen out of his shirt pocket and circled Kilneamh. "This is where the monastery was. The one I think where the manuscript, with the Selkie in the margins, originated." He circled other key points, like Ballrowan, where Gran's friend lived, the peat bog where the dirt originated and the standing stones where Maddy had had such strong visions.

The two spent the next half hour planning a route from the coast to Ballrowan, through Kilneamh, the site of the ruined monastery and historic tower. Maddy tapped her finger on the historic marker symbol showing the location of the ruins. "I think we should plan to spend some extra time here, maybe even start here. I've a feeling..." She lifted the jar and turned it slowly around as she watched the contents shift.

THEN

If Moira had to go into the village, or away from the croft for any reason, Ula would walk the short distance to Alfred's family and help out with the chores and the younger children. If Alfred was home, and not fishing with his father, he would often come down to Moira's and do small chores, repairs, or simply go for a walk with Ula. This way Ula was always in the company of another.

Alfred, while fitting splits into broken fencing at Moira's, wondered how long this would go on, how long she would be vulnerable. He glanced over at Ula, watching her comb and spin fleece. She sat in the sun, on a bench beside the door of the cottage. Her soft brown hair was pulled back into a rough braid. *The color of seal fur,* he thought idly. When they were wed—he and Ula had circled around that and hadn't committed to each other yet, but he was confident it would happen—then they would move away if they had to. Move somewhere where the Abbot nor his guards could find them.

This was not an easy path and not chosen lightly, for neither wanted to leave their homes. For Ula, there were concerns about Moira growing older, and of course, there was such love for the older woman who had nurtured her and been so accepting of who and what she was. For Alfred, it was the only home he'd known. His family, his life here was his world. He'd never imagined being anywhere else, working anywhere but the sea and their croft. To think of leaving it all behind was terrifying, but worse would be to see Ula taken, held captive. She'd already lost her freedom to be fully who and what she was, but to cut off any freedom whatsoever, to be held captive against her wishes, or worse, was beyond tolerating. He was sure it wasn't what God intended for any creature. That cursed Abbot... Alfred spat on the ground and wished it was the Abbot's face, as he was no man of God. May he rot in Hell.

For the Abbot, thoughts ran in the opposite direction. Yes, he assured himself, God intended the young fey one to be his. With his arms linked behind his back, the Abbot watched out his window as his guards rode through the gated archway and down the road. Soon, he thought, very soon. The young oblate, a monk in training, was a boy of about eight as best anyone could guess, who had been sent to the monastery for his training and schooling. He was the perfect bait for the trap that had been set. He had been told what to do with benevolent bribes, promises of riches from heaven that were underscored with terror and pain-filled threats to back up those bribes. Assured that the lad knew his role to play, the stage was set for success in this most delicate and exhilarating venture.

It was a market day in the village, and that meant the old woman would be out of the way. The wool she'd spun, and the ripened cheeses were most likely loaded in her cart by now, and she herself would be walking to the village alongside the lumbering oxen. It would take her the whole day there and then back. He knew that the girl, Ula, would normally go to the neighboring croft, but today there were other plans afoot to disrupt that scheme of things. His guards had been watching, reporting back on the meager attempts to keep her from her destiny. Didn't God help those who helped themselves? And so, he thought, he would help himself. Then with hands tucked neatly into the luxurious wool sleeves of his robe, as if hugging himself, he smiled.

Time eroded the sharp edge of anxiety as the days passed without threat from the Abbot or the nerve-wracking visits by his guards. It wasn't that the two families had become less guarded, but perhaps there was some easing of diligence. Moira and Ula had loaded the cart for market and the two would walk together as far as the neighboring croft. Ula would stay and help with chores there while Moira was away. Then a lamb escaped from its enclosure by the barn. Bleating and scrambling over this and under that, the two women tried to corner it but only made the lamb more frantic. Finally, Ula urged Moira to go ahead and leave, else she would be late to market. She would stay, let the lamb settle for a short bit, then entice it back into the enclosure with precious grain. Moira was uneasy about leaving, but the young woman assured her she'd stay within the confines of their yard then head straight to the neighbors once the lamb was settled back in its pen.

Ula had just secured the gate and was at last heading down the road to Alfred's family when she heard the pounding of feet behind her. She whirled, a walking stick held tightly. Alfred had insisted she always have it when out and about. A paltry weapon, but the best he could persuade her to carry. It was for her safety, he'd explained, and when she objected he added that it would relieve some of his worry to know she had it with her. Such a nuisance to carry and hard to remember to have it at all times, but more for his comfort than hers, she did as he wished.

Looking up the road she saw 'twas just a boy. One she did not recognize. Still, he wore the rough clothing of a farm lad, and couldn't be more than seven or eight. She wasn't a good judge of these things, but he looked younger than Alfred's brother, Ian, and certainly younger than his sisters.

She stood transfixed, wondering if she should run or stay and help. He didn't look dangerous, couldn't possibly be a threat, not like the Abbot's guards. Even when standing on the ground and not up on their impressive horses those men exuded a dangerous power. Here was just a lad for heaven's sake. Shorter and quite a bit younger than herself. She loosened her grip on the stout length of wood.

"Oh thank the Saints," the boy called out breathlessly. He bent near her, gasping to catch some air. "Can ye help?" He pointed towards the sea. "It's trapped, it is, in a net."

"Trapped?" Ula echoed, recalling vague memories of another time, on the beach with the sand gritty under her new-found feet. A seal trapped in a net. Moira had helped her release it. More than time spanned the distance to that moment. She was not that unformed, un-informed child anymore, no longer innocent in the ways of humankind. Yet, she could imagine the pain, the distress of the creature. Her kin, still, in some remote way.

The boy took her silence as hesitance. He would be punished severely, in this life and the afterlife, if he didn't fulfill his task. To get the girl down to the beach was what he'd been told then they would both be rewarded by God. He knew no more. But this part was, he understood clearly, was an imperative, for her well-being and for his.

"A seal, m'lady. I can't move it. Can ye not help me?" He begged, eyes wide, voice trembling. His fear was true as far as it went. Not so much for the creature they'd pulled ashore, although a tender heart might feel for it. He'd had no inclination nor consideration for tenderness, had been shown no such care himself for a long time. Protecting himself, food, shelter, his own well-being, these were his foremost concerns now.

Ula looked up the road, then down at the child, trembling. "Perhaps I should find one stronger than I?" she pondered.

The boy grabbed her hand and tugged. "No time, m'lady. Together we will be strong enough. I am sure." He started pulling her towards the path to the shore.

Ula once again looked down the road towards Alfred's family croft. The vision of the seal, caught, tangled and not being able to get back to sea filled her mind. It tugged at her. She knew what it was to not be able to return to the sea, to no longer be fully embraced by the water, loose the freedom to dive deeply, to be immersed in another existence all together. She allowed the child to set her course in the opposite direction of her intended journey. The coral and shell necklace around her neck jiggled against her skin as she kept pace with the child, striding towards the sea. It was the one Alfred had made for her. It gave comfort remembering his care for her. She would be back soon. She would be back in time, well before Moira returned, well before Alfred came back from fishing with his father.

Fondling the necklace of coral and shells, The Abbot held it up, letting it catch the candlelight. It would seem a poor cousin to the gold and gems alongside in the chest, but they represented a treasure beyond measure to the Abbot. She was his now. In the tower. Careful planning driven by what was surely divine intervention had given his guards a chance to capture the fey creature. The promises to the boy, and the fate of an old seal long forgotten. Some of the guards had crossed themselves when they'd brought her to him. Whispers of devil's work slithered in the stables and beyond. The Abbot cared not as he stroked the shells again. His wishes had been heard and answered, whether from above or below was no matter. It was enough that she was now his.

NOW

The day started out overcast and damp, but had cleared off to blue skies, at least for the moment, the mercurial weather so typical of a late summer day in the West country. Maddy and Bren planned an early start. They were just going to pack coffee, fruit and soda bread, figuring they'd catch a meal later on in the journey. Gran got wind of it, though, and insisted they have a good Irish breakfast to start the day right. Oatmeal, bread, eggs, beans, broiled tomatoes and rashers of bacon filled the small table in the kitchen.

"Gran, ye shouldn't have done all this," insisted Maddy.

"I'm over eighty years old, child. Ye'll not be tellin' the likes of me what I should and should na do so you may as well save your breath to cool yer porridge. You know a good meal will get you started right, and I'd as soon know you've been well fed afore you go on this venture. So, I'll do as I please and you best sit down and be sayin' thank you instead of fussing about." Gran was wiping her hands on her apron and then pouring the tea water into the pot. She popped the quilted cozy cover over it and looked up sharply as a car door slammed.

"It's your man." She smiled. "If I was younger, I'd give you a run for that one."

"I'd fight you for him." Maddy put up a fist and grinned at her Gran as she said it and looked up at the light tap on the door.

Bren opened it and stuck his head around it, sniffed deeply. "I think I've died and gone to heaven. You could smell the bread on the porch, and rashers to boot." He was rubbing his hands and grinning.

Gran looked right at her granddaughter. "Well, sure as I'm glad to see someone is appreciative of a good breakfast before a journey."

Bren looked at Maddy and then Gran with his brow furrowed. "Did I say the wrong thing?"

Gran said "no" and Maddy said "yes" at the same time.

This had Bren scratching his head. "Women—just when you think you understand them, it all goes betwixt and between." But he said it with a smile, which had both women laughing in kind.

"I just told Gran she shouldn't have done all the fuss about breakfast. Some coffee, fruit and bread would have been just fine."

"And I told Maddy that ye need to have fuel in the tank before a journey and she should just say thank you."

Maddy turned, gave her Gran a hug, kissed her soft weathered cheek and said, "Thank you."

"Now, that's more like it." Gran pulled out a chair, sat down and began helping herself to the hearty fare. Maddy and Bren joined her at the table, loading their plates as well.

They were on their way a little later than planned, but the Rover was finally heading towards the monastery ruins at Kilneamh.

As Bren was driving, he looked over to see Maddy biting her lip.

"Are you nervous?" Bren kept one hand on the steering wheel and reached over with the other to squeeze her hand.

"No." She shook her head. "No." She gave it more thought, was silent for a minute longer.

Bren glanced over at her again. "It's more being curious and a bit, hmmm, cautious isn't quite the word, it's more the anticipation, isn't it?"

She looked back over at him as she turned his hand, still in his, and gave it a squeeze.

He put both hands on the wheel again. Gray skies had moved in, with a bit of an ocean breeze, but the weather stayed mild. They had decided to head straight for the old ruins first, heeding Maddy's instincts. It was a pleasant drive and seemed like as good a place to start as any of the others highlighted on their map. The rest of the day would evolve from there.

The skeletal remains of the Abbey rose up out of the ground, old bones of a once mighty force in the land. When it was thriving, during the Middle Ages, rulers were far away and allegiances changed on a regular basis. It was the church, for good or ill, that anchored and governed the community, held it together.

They parked in the visitor lot, pea gravel crunching underfoot as they walked hand in hand towards the ruins. Maddy could feel the undercurrent, the deep hum of past activity, even the contemplative silence of the monks. Bren sensed her alertness, her awareness, and kept his hand securely in hers as they meandered through the arches of ancient doorways, past tumbled stone walls. Maddy would occasionally feel a chill and shudder. Bren would stop and look sharply over.

"I'm fine, 'tis nothing, or well, 'tis something, but nothing of consequence. A bit of a chill passing over, but not unusual in a place this old." She swept a hand out, encompassing the remnants of buildings and gardens. "As a history major, you've read enough to fill in the story. People worked here, loved here, died here, devoted their lives to God, or greed, or those more powerful. We know some facts from old documents, or as you've found, stories penned and illustrated into the edges of old manuscripts. An archaeologist, well they touch, dig, sift, trace. They take what's left of the physical evidence, the stones, doorways, walls, graveyard and with those artifacts fill in the missing bits and pieces to make a picture. For me, now, simply walking amongst what once was, it's not a picture or like a vision so much as that I simply sense the energy, the souls if you will, who once gave this all life."

She looked up then at the round tower as they were walking by. At 112 feet, it was the tallest stone structure still standing in all the country. The only entrance over twenty feet in the air. The tower was said to be even older than the Abbey itself. Perhaps built for fortification and protection, no one was quite sure. It outlived its creators, as well as those who'd walked by, lived here, chatted, gossiped, prayed, sold or traded goods as they did business under its shadow. It stood tall and strong.

She felt compelled to reach out to touch the rough stone surface.

Bren watched as the color drained from her face, held her as she went nearly limp in his arms. He managed to hold her and sink slowly to the ground. Leaning against the stone base of the tower, he sat with Maddy in his lap, her head on his shoulder.

"Maddy, are you with me? Can you hear me? Are you okay then?" He spoke urgently, but softly. Fortunately, it was a weekday, and very few tourists were out. They were alone on the back side of the tower, away from those few who were wandering the Abbey ruins.

Maddy shifted. Bren felt her surface as she slipped back to the present with a sigh. She took his hand and clasped it tightly. The vision, so fleeting and intense, fading now but still vibrating, echoing in her bones, her heart. "She's alone, and afraid. He put her in the tower. A treasure for his coffer, so to speak. The shells, the coral, they were hers, a gift that she wore around her neck. He took them." She spoke quickly, haltingly, like she was catching her breath.

"Jeysuz, you got all that, in what, less than a minute?" Bren's heart was still pounding, and levity was the only defense. The only response he could trust himself to make. He had told her he would be there for her, that he would be strong for her. Well, that was bullocks. He had felt helpless and on the verge of panic when Maddy started to slip away.

Suddenly, an old woman in a cloak of rough home spun was standing before them, looking down. "She'll be all right now, won't she? My girl. She had a good life with Alfred, but..." The woman looked up to the only window on that side of the tower, then out towards the West, towards the sea. "She always mourned the loss of her other self and of that which she held precious." Then she turned her gaze back to Bren and Maddy. "Ye'll return to her what was stolen, so she can be her true self again? Return to her the gift that was given in understanding and love? All taken in the name of purity and devotion. Bah!" The woman spat out. "But ye'll make it right now? Ye'll close it now?" The woman looked up again, her mind turned inward to distant memory. "She's waited a long time."

Bren looked up, startled, and seemed about to say something, but Maddy spoke first.

She smiled up at the woman. "And so have you waited," Maddy said softly, kindly. "It is a powerful energy, love that waits." She smiled. "Yes, we'll be getting it all back to her. You may rest yourself now."

The old woman nodded and smiled, then turned and seemed to melt into the sudden soft mist that arose around the ruins.

Bren blinked. "Who was that... was she... what girl... I mean what was that all about?" He couldn't quite make a complete thought, let alone a complete sentence. Couldn't quite put into words what his eyes and mind were still trying to reconcile.

"Ah, you saw her, did you?" Maddy started to get up, and as she knelt, put her hand on Bren's cheek. "She wasn't talking about the here and now as she wasn't from the here and now. She's connected to our Selkie girl."

Bren rubbed his hand over his face and shook his head slightly, then turned to look past the tower along the path the woman had gone. "You mean to tell me she wasn't real?"

"Now, that depends on how you want to define real. We both saw her, heard her. Is that not real?"

Bren shook his head. "But not real, like 'hey let's meet at the pub, have a pint and compare notes.'" He reached for Maddy's hand as she helped him up.

"No, luv, not quite like that."

"You mean to be tellin' me then," he said slowly, "I just saw and heard a ghost?" He stared down the path that passed along the tower.

"Some might call her a ghost. I prefer spirit, as that is essentially what she is or was. Energy connected by strong ties from the past to the here and now and not able to go far enough yet down their own road to let go. Love is a powerful force that can manifest in mysterious ways. She clearly loved our Selkie girl very much and won't rest easy until her Selkie girl can fully rest easy."

Bren's world shifted, then settled. Maddy could see the shift on his face, in his body language and realized he accepted. Just like that. Love indeed was a powerful force. This realization had her own world shifting and expanding to include accepting a love she never thought she'd have.

Taking both of Bren's hands, she placed one on her heart, laid her own hand over it and looked him straight in the eyes.

"Someone wanted to keep the Selkie girl as a treasure, as a prize, but real treasures in life are freely given, not held by bonds or walls. I love you Brennan O'Connor, and just to prove I am real and I mean it..." She paused for just a second, "...let's go to the pub, have a pint, and compare notes." She laughed full on as he grabbed her and swung her around.

THEN

Alfred and his father had gone out fishing, and Moira had gone into the village with cheeses to sell. As she went by, Moira had told Esthwyn about the lamb getting loose. Ula would be coming right along as soon as the young escapee was back in its enclosure. When Ula had not arrived at the neighboring croft promptly, the older girls had gone out see what was keeping her. Perhaps getting the lamb corralled was proving more difficult than imagined.

When Ula was nowhere to be found at her croft, they started a wider search. Recent rains had made the dirt of the rough road soft, and it is there where Elyn noticed footprints—distinctively two sets of prints. One set about her size, and one set smaller. Her skin prickled as she scanned the horizon. There was no sign of Ula. The girls raced all the way back to their own farm to alert the others that Ula was nowhere to be found.

When Alfred first heard the news he panicked, then imagined shaking Ula for being so, *what*, he thought, *careless?* No... he took a deep breath and reminded himself that she was always careful. She was not the one to blame for this disaster—it was another, one with more resources, more power. He wanted to storm the Abbey, confront the Abbot. His family, and Moira, equally alarmed, had to calm him down, and over pints of rough ale, bread and soup, the families made plans. With his prize secured, Moira felt, hoped, that Ula would not be harmed. At least not right off. He would want to savor his new acquisition, wouldn't he? Admire and congratulate himself on his cleverness?

Alfred's head took heed, but his heart hammered, his anger simmered just below the surface. He raised his ale and stared at those gathered around the table. "I'll warn ye now. If that walking pusillanimous piss pile of an Abbot dares to touch a hair on her head, dares to hurt her in any way..." He paused and took a gulp from his tankard. "...well,

I'd willingly send the old sot to hell and likely follow him there for the sin of killing a holy man. So be it." The tankard slammed down on the plank table.

Esthwyn gripped her son's shoulder. "We understand, and we all want her back safely, but we must take care. The Abbot has powerful alliances and followers. His guards had a part in following his orders, and will keep following without question, no matter how unholy his actions may be. We will find a way." Alfred's mother looked around the table at each one of them. Her husband, her daughters, even young Ian seemed to nod in agreement. Moira grabbed Esthwyn's hand and took Alfred's in her other hand.

"I am truly blessed to have such fine friends and neighbors. Surely the Gods will be on our side." No one quibbled about Moira's use of plural deities. Any and all Gods were welcome to aid in this desperate venture. "In the meantime, may they keep watch over our Ula, keep her safe and assure her we will bring her home." Then Moira smiled at Esthwyn.

"Then I think it may be time to plan a handfast union." Her smile turned towards Alfred. "Time goes by so quickly, so you must grab the good and the joy when you can, and hold it tight."

Alfred nodded, got nods around the table. "Then let's get her out, get her home and get us wed." He raised his tankard, tipped it up and drained it.

It was finally decided that Elyn, Alfred's oldest sister, would accompany her mother to market at the end of the week, and while Esthywn was trading goods or replenishing supplies, Elyn would listen for any gossip or hints as to Ula's whereabouts. The elite staff and guards at the Abbey would of course be sworn to silence, but the common folk, the unseen and unremarkable like the wash women, the butcher or his wife, the privy cleaners, they would see, would whisper.

When they were well out of town, and beyond suspicious eyes and ears, Elyn passed along to her mother what bits and pieces she had gathered. Some were disregarded, as the sources, mother and daughter agreed, were unreliable, or too fanciful. But once they sifted the wheat from the chaff, a direction, a plan could be formed.

"By all accounts, mother, there has been more activity around the old round tower. And Morag, the seamstress, says she is certain she saw, for the briefest moment, a young woman looking out the window. Do ye think it could be her?"

Esthwyn nodded. Yes, the round tower. "I've no doubt," was the tight reply. One door, over twenty feet in the air. Made of limestone, the tower rose to the heavens, tapered at the very top, with small windows dotting the upper half. It was more than ancient. A revered and sacred monument to power, protection, possession. "Ye've good ears and a sensible head on yer shoulders. We'll share this with the family and see what's to be done then."

A plan was formed. Not fool proof, as much would depend on fooling any guards or keepers of the tower. The lower half was generally used for storage of the tithed bounty for the Abbey and for the Abbot's use. Wheat, barley, oats, honey, ale kegs and the like would be hoisted up, then taken for storage floor by floor inside with the use of ladders.

Alfred, with a knife and a length of sisal rope, would snug inside a barrel. Purporting to be full of Mead it was to be offered to the Abbey. A bounty of their finest, their father would explain, as the honey had been so plentiful, to be given and to be shared with the Abbey inhabitants in exchange for extra blessings in the afterlife. Once hoisted up and through the door, Alfred would tap the lid from the inside to loosen it and pop it off. Then as necessary, would incapacitate the receiver of the barrel, then climb the upper ladders to find where Ula was kept. The two would then wait for the cover of dark. His father would have offered some of the mead to the keepers and guards to sample and stayed around to make sure they did, encouraging any and all to drink up and share the bounty. Plenty for the Abbey, and for the Abbot, he would assure them all, so no worries there.

Ula had shrunk against the wall when she heard the ladder creak, sensed someone coming. So far she had only been pulled towards the window a few times by servants or tower keepers when they brought her food. The Abbot would be below, his hands tucked in his sleeves as he would look up to her, nod and smile. It was not in a friendly way, but knowing, calculating, anticipating. It gave her shivers.

She gasped when she saw it was Alfred. He put a finger to his lips and came towards her, patting the air to signal her to sit. A length of sisal rope was looped over his shoulder, a dagger tucked in his belt. It looked wet and she could smell the earthiness of blood. She dared not ask but scanned him quickly to see if it was he who was hurt. He took her hands, squeezed them hard, then wrapped his arms around her. She held on tightly. Alfred was all right then.

"Ula," he whispered reverently. "Thank the Gods ye are here. We guessed, we hoped... are ye hurt at all..." He trailed off, his eyes hard. She shook her head, secrecy and silence imperative, and there would be time for words later.

He scanned the enclosure. Wooden plank floor. Three small windows set in the deep stone wall. There was a simple wooden pallet on one side with a wool blanket. A small table, and remnants of her midday meal—a wooden bowl, a cup. He went to the pallet, examined it carefully. Yes, he could lie down behind it, with the rope tucked in along his body, then have Ula rumple the blanket over the edge closest to the wall to cover him fully. He quietly explained the plan to her. She nodded, and although she smiled, it was her eyes he focused on. Ones that held his with trust and relief. Serious deep brown meeting his gray ones. She leaned into him, held his precious face in her hands, then kissed each cheek.

Quickly, succinctly, the two got to work quietly secreting him amid the tumble of the blanket and behind her bedding.

Her dinner was brought up the ladder and unceremoniously dumped from a bucket into her wooden bowl, a hunk of bread dropped on top and wine from a leather flask poured into her cup. Ula sat placidly, mumbling to herself, not saying a word to the guard. She tried to appear as if in contemplative prayer, in hopes the guard would leave her be and with his duty seen to would depart quickly.

The praying may have sped things along, but in truth, the keeper was already in a hurry. He assured himself the young woman wasn't going anywhere. Poor wee thing, he thought, as he reflected on her pious manner, her apparent innocence, while he nimbly, quickly, went back down the ladder against the outside wall. He gave a brief thought to the rumors, the whispers about her magikal nature, of the Abbot, and his plans for her. She looked like a sweet young thing to him, no sign of anything otherworldly. Ah well, there was no accounting for the likes of some, and he wasn't going to question the notions of the Abbot or the servants of God. Any concern he had was soon forgotten as his feet touched the ground and he headed toward the free-flowing Mead.

Ula could hear laughing, jesting and rough play outside. Drunken behavior. Moira had scoffed once, during a market trip, about the lazy men who were shouting and making lewd gestures outside the tavern. Too much drink and not enough brains, she'd said. Ale-brains she'd called them. Ula imagined it would be the same with the men below the tower. She could imagine they'd be snoring in tangled heaps before long. Good-the more ale-brained they got the better. Then she and Alfred would find their freedom.

THEN

Panic was not a feeling the Abbot was accustomed to. He had been rudely awoken in the early morning hours to be told the girl had escaped. Apparently a ruse and blundering keepers, fueled by an overdose of mead, allowed that young fisherman access to the tower. While he was stewing over that debacle and the loss of his precious treasure, his morning was further disturbed by a messenger.

A new Bishop had been appointed. If not for the documents presented upon his demand, he would have sent the man to be dealt with for lying. He could hardly grasp the insult, the shock. He'd sent the messenger away to be fed in the kitchens, barely keeping control of his temper, his outrage.

That appointment should have been his. Once the door had been shut, he gave vent to his anger and disbelief. With his body trembling he grabbed the silver grail he'd been drinking wine from and heaved it against the wall. He'd been so sure he'd be the one to fill that position and now he would have to bow and scrape to this charlatan. Adding insult to injury, the one who brought the news was one of the new Bishop's minions.

Later in the afternoon the messenger was ushered once again into the Abbot's private quarters. The new Bishop, he was informed, required a thorough accounting of all tithes and taxes taken in over the last several years. As he was one of the new Bishop's own clerks, and he would personally see to the review.

Caught off guard, the Abbot tried to think, to stall for time. He put on his most sincere smile and gestured to a chair, offering to share some wine. "This will take time, you realize," the Abbot said quickly, gesturing for the fellow to sit by the fire and rest a bit. The man sat heavily in the best chair, the Abbot's own favorite, although he deemed it prudent not to make a fuss about it. It grated, nonetheless. "I'll just go see the scribes now and let them know you'll be wanting to go over the accounts." He nodded and beamed. "Please make yourself comfortable."

Excusing himself, he bowed out of the room, carefully closing the heavy wooden plank door. Having been so sure he'd remain in charge, indeed that his reach, his prestige would only increase, there had been no perceived threat to his dealings. He'd not even considered for a moment that the books would be so scrutinized by anyone but himself or those loyal to him.

Before dawn the next morning, as he'd not slept, but had tossed and turned all night, he admitted that his carefully constructed world was rapidly unraveling. There had been pointed questions, discoveries of discrepancies, and much mumbling about repercussions, demotions, inevitably leading to excommunication. He'd tried to deflect much of the blame to his scribes, but they were poor attempts at what the Bishop's man saw as dissembling. The Abbot was ultimately responsible to oversee the work, therefore he was the one to shoulder the blame. He was the one who ultimately benefited from the mismanagement.

In the threshold between darkness and dawn the Abbot realized that there would be no forgiveness, no return to his former glory. There would be no time to recapture the girl or redeem the accounts to the Bishop's man's satisfaction. Saving himself was the primary concern now. He had to act quickly, yes, that was the only way. A carefully placed gold bauble or coin would assuredly get him safe passage on a merchant ship. He would escape censure and humiliation, start anew far away. Power and riches would, could, once again be his.

The sun was not even over the horizon when he decided he had no choice but to call for his guards. Hopefully they would still obey without question. "A horse and quickly," he demanded sharply when Muiredoch finally came to the door. It was an urgent mission of salvation and redemption. His. He grabbed his cloak and two large saddle bags, dumping into them what he could from his precious horde. He pulled out the seal skin and the shell necklace from the chest. He stroked the fur. If he couldn't have the fey creature, at least he would still have this part of her. Anger, lust, greed, all warred with the panic trembling through his being. The call for human survival pulls at the core, though. Self-preservation, with as much gilding greasing the way as he could manage, was the driving force now. He stuffed the skin and necklace into the top of one of the saddle bags. The bags were so laden that he could hardly carry them.

Thankfully there was a still full moon, just dipping towards the horizon, to help guide his way. It took Muiredoch and two other guards all they could do to heave the Abbot up on to the horse. The horse was skittish with the weight of the corpulent rider and his bulging saddle bags. The head guard stroked the horse's neck and handed the reins to the Abbot.

With reins held in a white-knuckled grip, he was off down the road towards the coast, with cloak flapping and the horse barely under control. The wind picked up and seemed to speed them on their way. Muiredoch stood and watched, shaking his head. He wished Godspeed for the horse, but he knew bargains with the devil never ended well. He would not send up a prayer for the Abbot; it would be a waste of time. Himself, well, he had been happy enough to look the other way, make a bit of extra coin, and enjoy the pleasures that came his way. He was only human and a man to boot. But the Abbot had crossed the line and was about to pay that horned piper for dancing to his tune. There would be a new Abbot and a new Bishop. They would both need guards and horsemen. Ah well, life went on, didn't it? Muiredoch turned and walked back to his quarters. He had a warm bed and a warm woman waiting. What more could a man ask for?

Not being an experienced rider, the Abbot held on to the reins for dear life, barely keeping the horse on the road. At one point the horse took off across an uneven bog field. He'd barely managed to stay on, as horse and rider bumped and bounced over the terrain. By the time he reached the coast one saddle bag was lost, the other only half full, as the contents had sloshed and spilled out along the rough and perilous ride.

Once arrogant and powerful, the Abbot was reduced to blubbering and begging. He was finally able to bribe the captain of a weathered ship to take him aboard. He hugged the last saddle bag to his body as they set sail. A few coins were all that were left in the bottom.

An unexpected storm arose, and the ship was lost at sea. There were no survivors. Legend had it that

the devil himself rode the towering waves, laughing
as the ship was sucked into the maelstrom.

NOW

At the pub, Maddy told Brennan what she felt they must do. It was really so simple. Give back to the sea what belonged to the sea, what had belonged to the Selkie girl. The soul can yearn for centuries, couldn't it? It was worth a try, and then perhaps, in doing so, what once was lost would be found.

They stood on the edge of the cliff. The sea was crashing and tumbling against the wall of rock below them. They'd never really be able to ascertain exactly which beach the story started on, so decided that any along a "best guess" area would do. The missing elements would be returned, and the sea would disperse as needed. Maddy lifted the jar and gazed at the contents. So many years, such a journey, a simple jar of dirt with an amazing story.

Bren was right behind her, his arms encircling her shoulders, holding her securely. He kissed the top of her head.

"Ready?" he asked softly.

"More than," she answered just as softly.

She unscrewed the lid and in one smooth gesture, extended her arm and flung the contents into the wind and over the edge, drifting down to the water below. The empty jar in one hand, her other holding on to Bren's at her shoulder, they watched as the wind sent the contents of the jar out, settling on the sea. They couldn't see the fine grains but rather imagined the ocean waves were pulling them farther and farther out with each sweep of the shore.

"Just like that, then?" Brennan asked softly against her ear. "Done now. I feel a sense of peace. Do you feel it as well?"

Maddy nodded, leaned her head against Bren's shoulder, squeezed his hand on her shoulder and let her mind drift. *Be well, be whole, be free. Blessed be*, she thought.

As they watched the tide go out, Maddy thought she saw a seal pop its head up and look towards the cliffs.

ACKNOWLEDGEMENTS

The story may be intriguing and the characters memorable but they wouldn't be brought to life without the support and help of friends and family. My heartfelt thanks to the West Windsor writer's group as well as Liz, Sharry, Jane, my daughter Dana, my sister Barbara and so many others who read drafts, listened, encouraged, nagged and inspired me to get Madeline's story in print.

Cliched but true—I couldn't have done it without any of you!

About the Author

With extensive travel experience in the British Isles and her own life deeply rooted in Vermont, Penelope Bliss sees magic everywhere. She feels that relationships and finding romance have their own magical nuances that intrigue and validate our very existence as well as teach us to be open to the new, the unexpected.

Being creative, in the garden, in her artwork, or in writing has always been a vital part of Penelope's life. She has written, illustrated and published one children's book, *Joleen Makes Room*, about a confident cat. *Lost and Found* is her first novel but be assured that Madeline Murphy is just settling in as an enduring character. A sequel, *Tossed and Found,* is in the works, featuring Madeline and her unique talent to solve unusual mysteries.

The Next Intriguing Madeline Murphy Mystery

Brennan's sister, Erin, discovers a medieval ring and a new love—potentially a forever love. But the ring comes with a curse that disrupts Erin's hopes of a future with Hayden Whittaker, a wealthy, handsome museum curator of historic artifacts and antiquities. Madeline, with her unique insight, and Brennan, along with Erin and Hayden, join forces in the daunting and dangerous task of breaking the ancient curse.

www.ingramcontent.com/pod-product-compliance
Lightning Source LLC
Chambersburg PA
CBHW061547210726
48287CB00006B/2104